I0535970

Copyright © 2012/2021 by Jannette Quackenbush
ISBN-10:1-940087-06-6
ISBN-13:978-1-940087-06-1

This is a work of fiction. Names, characters, places and incidents either are the product of the author's imagination or are used fictitiously, and any resemblance to any actual persons, living or dead, events, or locales is entirely coincidental. This book was printed in the United States of America.

Table of Contents

Allen County

Athens County

Belmont County

Delaware County

Fayette County

Franklin County

Gallia County

Hancock County

Henry County

Lucas County

Marion County

Muskingum County

Perry County

Pike County

Allen County

Old Farm Spring
*Between North Elizabeth
and North Union Streets
Lima, Ohio 45801
40.761719, -84.104988*

Little Lima Light

A ghost once walked this street in Lima.

During the autumn and winter of 1890, some traveling along Elizabeth Street in Lima between eleven and midnight would see a bright light bobbing about. It appeared like a lantern's flame, was held steady at about the height of a man's shoulders, and worked slowly back and forth as if held by unseen hands. It would eventually come to a stop at a spring located on a farm before vanishing. After a few moments, it would reappear at the spring and follow the same path from which it had come.

Some followed the light but could not explain its presence. Several waited until light snow, expecting to discover footprints. Yet none were left behind. Many believed the light was the flicker of a lantern light—years earlier, an old man living nearby who often visited the spring died.

State Hospital Cemetery
The Grave of Celia Rose
E Chapman and Bible Road
Lima, Ohio 45801
40.773666, -84.094852

Grave Walker

The grave of Celia Rose.

In 1896, 23-year old Celia Rose fell in love with a neighbor boy who did not return her affections. Understanding that their daughter only had the intellectual ability of a small child, when she began to hound the young man for affection, her mother and father sat her down and firmly forbade she visit him again.

Angry, Celia added the poison Rough on Rats to their morning cottage cheese and poisoned her mother, father, and brother. Celia was found guilty in court, but the judge acquitted the young woman for mental illness. Instead, authorities sent Celia to Lima State Hospital in Allen County, where she died in 1934. She was buried in the state hospital cemetery. Those traveling past the old cemetery have seen an older woman walking among the graves and recognize her as Celia Rose.

Celia Rose.

Athens County

Concord Church Cemetery
12272 Concord Church Road
Glouster, Ohio 45732
39.450891,-82.050834

Baby Rocker

The Wolf family moved from Pennsylvania to Athens County in the late 1700s to farm the bottomlands of the Bryson Branch of Federal Creek, and they lived in the community for many generations. There is a small church with a cemetery that became the final resting place for their dead. Passersby have seen the spirit of an old lady sitting atop one gravestone. She is holding a restless baby and rocking it back and forth. A lone ghostly wolf also guards the cemetery, never crossing the boundary within.

West State Street Cemetery
West State /Cemetery Streets
Athens, Ohio 45701
39.332356, -82.105851

Weeping Angel

About the time the first settlers came to Athens in the late 1700s, a cemetery was built on a hillside. Over the years, veterans from the Revolutionary War and Civil War would be buried here along with members of Congress, a baseball player, and even a notorious murderer. Some of the earliest headstones have crumbled away, surrendering to time and harsh weather. Nobody seems to know or care who was buried beneath them, except for one.

There is a statue of an angel at the entrance that watches over those whose markers are long gone. She is holding a book, and it is thought that she is writing the names of the unknown within the pages so that the living do not forget them. Those passing by have seen her weeping, moving, and even fluttering her wings. Orbs of light hover and dance around the angel, and some believe they work their way to each lost grave.

Anthony Cabin
Hocking College
3301 Hocking Parkway
Nelsonville, Ohio 45764
39.440046,-82.218075

The Haunted Cabin

The haunted cabin.

There is a haunting in Nelsonville. It centers around an old cabin built by John and Martha Anthony over 190 years ago on land outside Union Furnace. It would still be quietly settled there along with its haunting if it were not for the Nutter Brothers strip mining on Loomis Road in the 1970s. The company was going to demolish the building before they dynamited and bulldozed the property to get to the coal beneath. But the Anthony family, who had lived in the home for generations, donated the building to Hocking College in 1977 as part of a historical teaching complex.

The cabin is unique—a duplex found more commonly in close-knit Appalachian communities than anywhere else. It offered separate quarters for two generations of the family—the parents lived on one side and their grown child and family on the other. A total of four generations have lived in the home since 1830. It is worth saving. There is a ghost. With all the mamas and daddies, kids, aunts, uncles, and grandparents living and loving and sometimes dying at the cabin, it was not at all surprising, even to the family, that somebody decided to stick around after death.

It was not just the family who knew about the ghost. When dismantling the building, some employees of the strip-mining company refused to help take down the home. They had seen the ghost on occasion rambling around outside the building—one even going as far to divulge that while he was patrolling the area around 2 a.m., he watched in astonishment as a tall, white ghost drifted from within the cabin and worked its way around the building.

Another offered this up about the ghostly presence before the cabin's move to the campus: "I don't want to go up there and tear down that guy's home." But they did tear it down and put it back together at the college to save it. It was not too long ago that folks would place an evergreen on the highest beam of a new wood home. It appeased the spirits that came with the trees, gave them a place to live, and made for less mischief for those residing there. During the reconstruction of the Anthony Cabin on the lot at Hocking College, someone added an evergreen sprig. It must have fallen off because the spirit shows up occasionally. Over the years at Hocking College, staff and visitors have watched as doors open and close on their own. Ghostly footsteps creep across the floor, and voices from the home's long past linger in the air. Sometimes, a pale figure drifts from within the cabin in the dark of night and roams the grounds.

The Athens Asylum and Cemeteries
The Ridges Cemetery Trail
Athens, Ohio 45701
39.322957, -82.113671

What Margaret Schilling Left Behind

The old asylum

The sprawling old asylum is a familiar sight in the college town of Athens. It has been a solid fixture in the region since 1874 as a mental health hospital. The grounds were filled with gardens, ponds, and fountains in earlier years, and the property and buildings were set up like a working farm. Patients worked in these areas, including orchards, greenhouses, dairy, and piggery.

It housed civil war soldiers, violent criminals, the old, the disabled, the sick, and even young children. Doctors committed patients for many reasons, some appearing ridiculous by our standards now: laziness, disappointed love, female disease, mental excitement, cold, epilepsy, hysteria, asthma. Then it was called the Athens Lunatic Asylum, and its name changed many times over the years. Now, much has been refurbished and houses the Kennedy Museum-Linn Hall and other Ohio University offices called The Ridges. Trails are meandering through the woods and orchards and cemeteries.

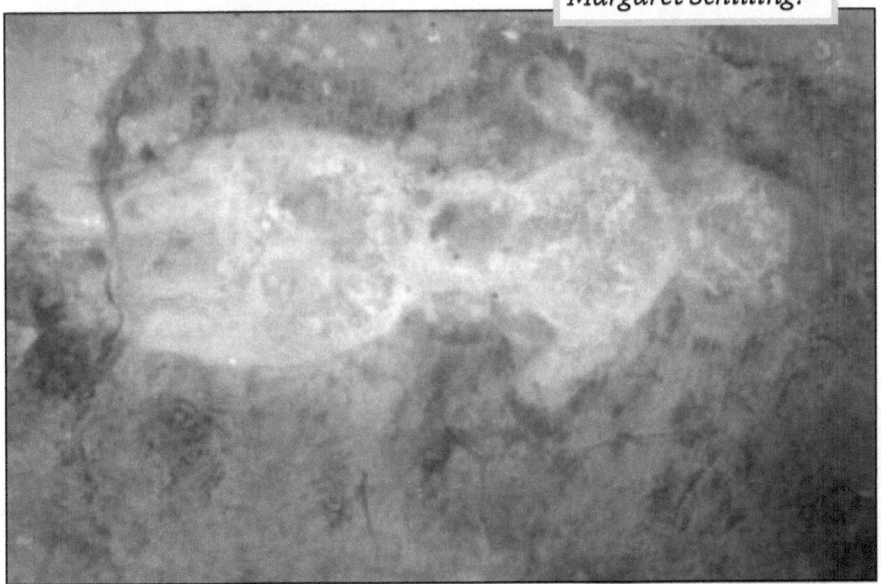

Margaret Schilling.

Over the years, legends of hauntings have arisen on the grounds of the old asylum. Students, staff, and professors have told stories of ghostly screams, objects moving in rooms, and chatter within the building. It was a hospital, so within the walls, there were many deaths. One strange passing occurred in the late 1970s when a patient's body, 54 -year-old Margaret Schilling, was discovered in an unused ward 42 days after disappearing. The nurses had believed the woman had walked away from the hospital grounds.

Instead, she had wandered to an upper floor and inadvertently locked herself in a room. A maintenance worker discovered her. A clear imprint of her body remains on the floor today, the oozy remnants of body fluids that cannot be scrubbed away. Some say that the body imprint is not all that lingers from Ms. Schilling. Her ghost also hovers in the room nearby.

The grounds have three cemeteries. All of these can be visited during daylight via a well-maintained trail system. Screams, whispers, shadow figures, and chatter are reported around these old burial places of the asylum.

Belmont County

***Louiza Catherine Fox
Murder Site***
*Twp Hwy 546 B (Starkey Road)
Barnesville, Ohio 43713
40.104476,-81.174702*

Silent Louiza

On a bare hillside of old strip-mined land at Egypt Valley Wildlife Area, there sits a lone stone with an inscription. It marks the murder place of Louiza Fox. And some have seen her ghost silently pacing there. *Here is her story—*

Thirteen-year-old Louiza Fox was returning to her family farm near Sewellsville on a late afternoon in January 1869. The pretty young girl was a live-in housemaid for the Hunter family, owners of a local coal mine.

One of the miners also in Hunter's employ, 22-year-old Thomas Carr, had been pursuing the little girl relentlessly since the previous autumn. He had, several times, accompanied her from work to home. John Fox, Louiza's father, questioned Carr with a wary eye, but the miner insisted he only walked with Louiza to watch over her because of her tender age. Louiza refused any idea of courting the older man again and again. However, it was brought to her father's attention by Louiza herself that Carr had asked her to marry him some weeks later. The child asked her father to please refuse the peculiar, threatening, and unpleasant man; she had no interest in him.

When Carr confronted the father to ask her hand in marriage, John Fox kindly excused the askance, telling Carr that Louiza was too young. Perhaps in maybe two or three years if he proved himself worthy by keeping a job and purchased a bit of land AND if the young woman, who would be closer to marriageable age, was willing, he could ask for her hand again. But during the last weeks of January, knowing her temporary time working at the Hunter family's home was coming to an end, Carr's menacing presence had increased. Although Louiza and her father both thwarted continued advances and gift-bestowing by Carr, his stalking had come to a head on that fateful day as he followed her from room to room, asking her to marry him. Noting Carr's strange behavior, Louiza's employer tried to persuade the young girl to stay at the Hunter house for her safety until they could take her home by horseback.

But really, her walk was not too far away. Her home and other family members' homes were just off what is now Starkey Road and near the Egypt Valley Wildlife Area. Carr was odd and argumentative. He was not working and was a braggart. He offered meager social skills, but they would have never imagined him a horrible monster that would stalk and murder a child.

Such, in the tiny tightknit community seemingly protected from the evils of the outside world, no one, not even her family, appeared to surmise the extent of evil broiling inside this madman. But he had already begun to believe the polite rebuttal offered by her father was just a formality in asking for her hand in marriage. In his irrational state, Carr thought that the well-mannered rebuffs from the sweet little girl were only to please her father, and she was simply hiding whatever love or lust she felt for him behind her modesty. It was, in fact, her 6-year-old brother, Willy, sent to escort her home when worried about her welfare returning from the Hunter home. Carr had demanded for the last time to speak with John Fox and had threatened the man to give his daughter's hand to him in marriage —or else. John refused him.

Probably out of youthful innocence of Carr's intentions, Louiza refused Missus Hunter's advice for her to remain in the house that day. When her brother arrived to walk home with her, she did set out around four or five in the afternoon. After several attempts of Carr to waylay Louiza on her path home, she tried desperately to allude him along the isolated roadway by running at some points.

Then as Louiza and her little brother passed a small chestnut orchard a stone's throw from home, Carr made his move and crept from beside a fence by the trees and into their path. After sending the younger brother on his way, Carr asked the girl to marry him once again. She refused, telling him that she was far too young to be wed. He then pulled a razor from his pocket, tossed her by one shoulder to the ground, and slit her throat.

By the time her father had hastened to the spot, he had found young Louiza lying dead in a small ditch by the road where Carr had dragged her during the short struggle. Carr was hunted down and eventually apprehended and hanged.

The marker where she was murdered.

There is a stone in Belmont County tucked into the Egypt Valley Wildlife Area marking the place where Carr murdered Louiza. It is not the only sign Carr killed her there—her ghost walks the grassy hillside. She is silent because the razor to her throat spoilt any ghostly screams for help.

Not far away is Louiza Fox 's Grave at Salem Cemetery where she is also said to wander in ghostly form—
Salem Cemetery Barnesville, Ohio 43983
(40.089460, -81.153695)

Delaware County

Henry Street
S Henry Street
Delaware, Ohio 43015
40.295976, -83.064468

The Red Slipper Murder

Henry Street in Delaware where a ghostly murder victim walks.

A squirrel hunter found the mysterious girl's body clad only in a flannel nightgown and red, one-strap slippers on September 18th, 1953. She was dumped near a deserted roadside along Route 53 in Wyandot County 3 miles north of Upper Sandusky, her face so severely crushed that it was unidentifiable. Local police traced the serial number inside the red slippers from Columbus shoe manufacturer Prima Footwear that distributed their products to a department store in White Plains, New York. Unofficial police reports from White plains showed a young woman, blue-eyed Cynthia Pfeil, had been missing since August 24th. With a photo of Cynthia in hand, police marched to the department store where the slippers had been purchased.

One clerk recalled selling the shoes to the girl only two days before she disappeared. Shortly after, the police headed to the home of Cynthia's parents, who stated they were unsure of their daughter's whereabouts. However, they believed she was with a boyfriend, Roger Schinagle, whom they did not approve of, but Cynthia had met when they attended the university together a year ago. Police brought in slim, clean-cut, and sandy-haired Roger Schinagle, age 19 and a Ohio Wesleyan sophomore, for questioning shortly after; he hardly fit the profile of a murderer. But they did not know his dark and jealous side. Cynthia had returned home after her freshman year and began work in Cleveland. Roger worked for a trucking company, and when he was not in school, he drove through Cleveland to see her.

Cynthia snuck down to see Roger in Delaware, divulging she had to tell him something. He set her up in the equipment shed at the south athletic field on the campus because she could not afford a hotel room. Roger would not allow her to leave as he did not want anyone to know she was there and demanded she not leave the shed. But Cynthia did not heed his words, grew restless at being cooped up, and wandered out to the field. A groundskeeper spotted the girl and hastily informed Roger that he knew she was staying there. Angry, Roger returned, dragged Cynthia back inside the small building, and beat her so furiously with a lead pipe, he killed her. He then dumped her body in an isolated area 35 miles away from campus.

Roger Schinagle went to prison for ten years and was released. Her family buried 19-year-old Cynthia in White Plains. She had been two months pregnant at the time of the murder, and Roger admitted the child was his own. But her story is far from over. Cynthia walks Henry Street near her murder site in a flannel nightgown and red, one-strap slippers. Some have even heard her wailing as she strolls along the route.

Blue Limestone Park
6 King Ave
Delaware, Ohio 43015
40.300383, -83.078474

Spectral Lights at Blue Stone Quarry

Blue Limestone Park.

Some who visit Blue Stone Quarry in Delaware have seen lights easing along a railway nearby. Others have reported strange whispers and tiny, pale orbs bobbing around in the park, especially near a tunnel. It is somewhat of a mystery pinpointing the exact cause of the spectral lights and ghostly sounds.

Many attribute these strange sights and noises to the deaths in the quarries—in 1961, a man drowned swimming with friends in the cool waters. In 1967, two Ohio Wesleyan college students discovered a 19-year-old nurse's aide's partially dressed body floating in the water at the park.

Others have a different opinion. They believe nearby train wrecks have left an apparition or two. One occurring northeast of town was a horrific crash only two days before Christmas in December of 1934. A train speeding through Delaware filled with holiday passengers and mail collided with a second train just past a curve outside town. When the midnight No. 42 sped around the cutoff just outside Delaware, it rammed into the third car back from Central's eastern mail locomotive, No. 28. Two of the locomotives turned over in a ditch. Three railroad employees died.

Perkins Observatory
3199 Columbus Pike
Delaware, Ohio 43015
40.251134,-83.055739

The Overseer

Perkins Observatory.

Hiram Perkins.

Occasionally, those visiting Perkins Observatory see a tall, lanky figure walking around the building and grounds on clear, starry nights. Then the form suddenly vanishes. Nowadays, few know to whom the ghostly form belongs; he died nearly a hundred years ago. But in the late 1800s, he was a solid figure in the community. His name was Hiram Perkins.

Hiram Perkins grew up on a pig farm in Madison County, then went to Ohio Wesleyan University, where he graduated with a degree in Math and Astronomy. He taught for a while at the college, then as the school's budget began getting cramped during the Civil War, he left his job so another faculty member could have his position.

He returned home to help his family raise hogs to sell to the Union Army, and being frugal, made a fortune from this venture. After the war, Hiram returned to his teaching at the university and later on bequeathed a lifetime of savings and investments to build Perkins Student Observatory. He died at the age of 90 before the building was completed. But he returns now to oversee the grounds along with the observatory.

Schines Strand Theatre
28 East Winter Street
Delaware, Ohio 43015
40.299969,-83.066517

Mischief

Years ago, the Strand Theatre featured vaudeville shows with suited ushers seating the patrons. Later, the theatre would add feature films to its venue and become a part of the Schine chain of theatres. Now, it offers movies—and ghosts. Plenty of children have visited this theatre over the years, and a few have returned with a bit of mischief. Staff have items mysteriously moved from one place to another, doors slam shut on their own, and the noise of children playing fills the air—when no live children are around. Near the projection booth, a spirited boy in knickers and suspenders hangs around before disappearing.

Fayette County

Ghormley Road Bridge
Township Highway 156
Greenfield, Ohio 45123
39.409241,-83.383534

Crybaby Bridge

Ghormley Road Bridge.

At one time, the Detroit, Toledo, & Ironton Railroad passed through Ghormley's Station between Washington Courthouse and Greenfield. It was a flag stop station where trains only stopped if signaled. After many years, the trains stopped coming through, the rails were pulled, and only a farmstead or two remained of the tiny town.

But sometime during its existence, a woman was fleeing from her burning home with her baby in her arms. As she ran across the Ghormley Road bridge, the child slipped from her arms and tumbled into the creek. Before she could retrieve him, the infant drowned. In a hysterical fit, she tied a sheet around the bridge and hanged herself. Some people have seen the ghost of the woman roaming the bridge after they pass by the old rail town, and others have heard the baby's crying.

Cherry Hill
OH-38 and Co Hwy 113
Yatesville, Ohio 43106
39.665178,-83.441091 to
39.682784,-83.415291

Headless Horseman of Cherry Hill

A headless horseman once stalked residents along State Route 38 near Yatesville. One pair of early tavernkeepers living on a small rise called Cherry Hill were notorious counterfeiters and ruffians. When a ghostly horseman began to show on the hill near their home, rumors wafted through the community that the innkeepers had murdered a federal agent secretly investigating their illegal activities. The husband killed the federal agent, cut off his head, and dumped his body in a well.

They found the agent's horse tied to a tree. When the wife discovered her husband had murdered the man, he tried to kill her too. She turned him into the police. Later, when a farmer was plowing, several skeletons were found on Cherry Hill where the inn once stood and the dead horseman rode.

Franklin County

**Scioto River Near
North Bank Park along Lower
Scioto Greenway**
312 W Long Street
Columbus, Ohio 43215
39.964730, -83.015067

Bloody Island

Once near the location North Bank Park stands today, Bloody Island is gone, destroyed when the Army Corps of Engineers widened the Scioto River to aid in flood prevention. However, ghosts remain.

There once was a small island just before the meeting of the Olentangy River with the Scioto River in Columbus. On the shoreline close by, people have long told of hearing moans and cries. There is an explanation for the sounds—

The island went by many names—Brickell Island after the settler and landowner John Brickell, and then Willow Island for the trees that grew abundantly on its banks. But it would also gain a ghastly name later—*Bloody Island.*

During the late 1700s, the colonial governor of Virginia, Dunmore, declared war with the Indians as they attacked settlers along the Ohio River. He led a large army into Ohio, stopping in Circleville to camp. He then sent Colonel William Crawford and a few hundred riders to invade Indian villages along the Forks of Scioto, near Columbus' Arena District today.

As the militia came upon the village, it was clear that few men were around as they were on their first fall hunt. So the soldiers struck with a vengeance and easily so, outnumbering the old men, women, and children. With wild abandon, they rushed upon the unarmed villagers and began firing. The villagers, in a panic, started to flee in all directions. One woman was able to snatch up her five-year-old child and carry him to the safety of the willow-covered island nearby. She was quickly shot down and killed, but the child escaped into the trees and concealed himself in the hollow of a sycamore.

When the warriors returned two days later, they discovered the little one still safely tucked into its grasp. Yet, most of their family members were murdered and left dead on the shores covered in blood. Many years would pass where nobody lived near the banks. Then as the land was settled, and later the city grew, the gruesome cries of those villagers who died there began to echo eerily in the wind.

You can access the Lower Scioto Greenway at North Bank Park and walk near the area of the long-gone island, although it may be difficult to see the waterway seasonally.

North Bank Park hike along Lower Scioto Greenway

311 W Long Street

Columbus, Ohio 43215

39.965347, -83.010015 to

39.965635, -83.015288

Along the Olentangy River
Columbus, Ohio 43215

British Island

Up the Olentangy River, there was once a small island. During the War of 1812, British soldiers defeated at the Thames River in Canada were kept prisoner here. Muddy and flooded, it was a miserable place for the men. Sometime during their stay, some soldiers decided to escape and began to swim across the river. They were almost to the banks when their captors shot them dead. For years after, witnesses heard splashing, yells, and groans creeping from the water where the men were murdered.

Camp Chase Cemetery
Sullivant Avenue
Columbus, Ohio 43204
39.943881,-83.075953

Veiled Lady of Camp Chase Cemetery

Camp Chase during the Civil War.

In Columbus, the Hilltop subdivision was once a training encampment for Union recruits called Camp Chase and later a prisoner of war camp holding enlisted Confederates. When the camp closed after the war, Quakers purchased the property as a settlement. Within a couple of years of the end of the war, the structures for the camp were dismantled.

The Confederate prisoners' cemetery, then on a lonely dirt road called Sullivant's Free Pike and near the area of the camp pest house, was abandoned and left overridden with weeds.

Camp Chase Cemetery—late 1800s.

Travelers passing by noted a lady in a gray dress and veil walking through the cemetery during those years. She was heard crying softly to herself and, at times, tossed flowers and petals on the graves. Most went on, leaving her politely to her grief. However, others whispered shaming words about her; the wounds from the war were still fresh, and some held disdain for the dead rebels there. But few knew the mysterious woman's identity until many years later.

Louisiana Ransburg Briggs, a young woman from Missouri, was sent to be schooled at Ohio Wesleyan to save her from the ravages of war in the south. Some classmates disliked her for being openly supportive of the south. She met her future husband, Joseph Briggs—prominent Franklin County landowner, while at the school, marrying him in 1867 at age 17.

A few years after her marriage, she discovered the cemetery. For ten years, she courageously scattered flowers amongst the neglected cemetery wearing a veil to hide her identity and save her husband's reputation from being marred. Over the years and with the aid of William Knauss, a former Union soldier, the cemetery was cleaned, and memorial services began.

Camp Chase Cemetery today.

Camp Chase was, like most prison camps, overcrowded. Some of the confined soldiers there died from smallpox (many in an 1863 - 1864 epidemic), cholera, and starvation. Over 2,168 Confederate soldiers were buried in the Camp Chase Cemetery.

She still walks among the graves. Passersby have seen a ghostly woman walking among the graves in dark clothing and veil. When they pause in their steps to ponder her strange garb, she disappears.

Central Ohio Fire Museum
260 N. 4th Street
Columbus, Ohio 43215
39.968117, -82.996956

Whinnies in the Hall

Back in the early days of Columbus, volunteer firefighters consisted of twelve men, ages 15 to 50. They would divide into groups at a fire to do everything from guarding the property on fire to forming a bucket brigade, passing buckets from one to another until the last bucket holder could reach the fire.

As the city grew, so did the need for faster and more efficient equipment. To get volunteers, city authorities began paying the men in order of how quickly they showed up at the scene of the fire to help—five dollars to the first fireman to arrive, four dollars to the second man, and three dollars to the third. With the purchase of a steam fire engine in the mid-1800s and the need to house horses to pull it, the city hired a paid fire crew. Engine House Number 16 was an active City of Columbus firehouse from 1908 to 1981.

It was the last engine station built to house horses as the Columbus Fire Department began to transition to motorized equipment over the next ten years. It would be December of 1919 before the department's last horses were retired from this very building. Now, the structure is a fire museum and haunted, too, by the horses that once called it home. Those within have heard neighs, snorts, and whinnies echoing eerily through the halls. However, those who worry about the ghostly horses not receiving proper attention need not fret. The spirit of one of the first captains to work there, George Dukeman, haunts the museum. He was a meticulous man and made it painstakingly clear everything should be cared for, cleaned, and in its place. He was known to be particular about making sure someone tidied up the equipment in the upstairs. People have heard the sounds of the captain still working and singing to his chores. Lights go on and off, and shut doors bang open wide.

Livingston Park Cemetery
(aka: Columbus City Cemetery, East Graveyard, Old East Graveyard, South Graveyard)
Children's Hospital/ Livingston Park
S 18th Street
Columbus, Ohio 43205
39.953043, -82.976486

Old East Graveyard—The Unclaimed

The area of an old cemetery, now gone.

An aged cemetery lies hidden beneath a park in Columbus. It began as 11 1/4 swampy acres on Livingston Avenue and Eighteenth Street in 1839, and within ten years, the city added a dead house to store corpses until burial. The city sold lots in the front to residents, while the rear became a burial ground for the public, which from 1862 to 1863, prison authorities had 22 Confederate prisoners from Camp Chase interred here.

People like James Broome were buried in the lot too. He left his family in Pennsylvania, got drunk on bad whiskey, and died during his stay one night in jail. His body was taken to the dead house, but nobody ever claimed him. Nobody claimed Birdie May either. She was buried at the cemetery too in 1871, a young woman who boarded at what a newspaper referred to as "Sue Stump's disrespectable house on Strawberry Alley." Birdie returned one late evening, cried out, "I'm dying, I'm dying!" and fell back to the floor dead. James Taylor was in his early twenties and worked on a canal boat before he ended up in the old yard for the dead. One afternoon he decided to cool off in the Scioto River, but a cramp seized him; he disappeared under the water and never came back up on his own. His family hailed from England, and, being mid-August, the body needed to be entombed quickly, so he was buried in the old cemetery with all the others unclaimed.

By 1873, the cemetery name had been changed from South Cemetery to East Cemetery. It had fallen into disrepair with broken fences and headstones, uncut grass, and only the poor and paupers were laid to rest beneath the ground. It was closed in the mid-1870s and declared a park, South Park, and later renamed Livingston Park. Some of the 2,344 known graves were removed. Still, the actual number of the dead beneath the soil would never be known as many were buried there without approval. Some stones were still remaining into the late 1950s when workers dumped them to support the banks of Alum Creek during a flood. Many years have passed since the graveyard was filled with the newly departed. Occasionally those enjoying themselves at Livingston Park or visiting Children's Hospital hear weird voices for which they cannot account. They see strangely dressed people strolling through the grass and along the street, then they disappear from sight.

Columbus Public Health Department
240 Parsons Avenue
Columbus, Ohio 43205
39.959174,-82.980628

Those Who Decided to Stay

The building between 1900 and 1920. Image: Library of Congress.

The sound of ghostly feet pound down the hallways of the three-story Columbus Public Health Department. Doors slam and specters peer around corners. It sounds terrifying, until you learn the noise comes from mischievous children who once filled the building and not murderous phantoms. From 1874 to 1953, the structure was the Ohio State School for the Blind, and those haunting it are the children who learned and stayed there. Those, that is, who decided to stay.

Ohio Statehouse
1 Capitol Square
Columbus, Ohio 43215
39.961481,-82.999091

Unfinished Dance

Kate Chase, right, her father Salmon and sister.
Image: Library of Congress.

Salmon Chase, a Cincinnati lawyer in the mid-1800s, was the elected governor of Ohio with aspirations of becoming president. Because Chase was without a wife, his doting daughter Kate became his official hostess at fifteen in Columbus while he was the governor and later in Washington after he was appointed treasury secretary.

She was well-qualified; after rivaling for her father's affections at age eight with his third wife, Kate was sent away to the country's most elite and exclusive private girls schools and taught all the graces of high society young women.

At one event in the Statehouse in 1859, legends are passed down that Abraham Lincoln, not yet president, and his wife, Mary, came to visit the Statehouse on a political campaign to begin working on common objectives with those who might be political rivals like Chase. During the evening festivities, which included a lavish Statehouse military ball, Kate (who was known to be quite flirtatious) advanced upon Abraham Lincoln and persuaded him to accompany her on the dance floor. A furious Mary Lincoln, who had met her husband at a cotillion herself in Springfield, Illinois, immediately stopped the band and escorted her husband from the floor. For the remainder of the two women's lives, they would each take turns refusing to attend certain events together. After death, Kate may have returned to cast a final blow—her ghost, along with the dead president Lincoln, has been seen promenading across the Statehouse floor, finally finishing their dance.

Little Pennsylvania Cemetery
7700 London-Groveport Road
Grove City, Ohio 43123
39.850457,-83.201194

The Woolly-Booger

Little Pennsylvania Cemetery has also been called Woolyburger Cemetery, Woolybooger Cemetery, and Willie Butcher's Cemetery.

Big Darby Creek runs 84 miles, and along its route, it passes through the town of Darbydale. Just outside Darbydale is an ancient cemetery, Little Pennsylvania Cemetery, where people like the Atheys, Hambletons, and Bouchers have found their final resting place. As small as it is with a little over 200 graves, the cemetery still has many stories conjured up about it for over half a century.

Some spoke of a Bigfoot seen in the area—as they call them in the south, a Woolly Booger or hairy man. Others whispered that a man butchered his family and killed himself, only to return from the grave as a boogeyman. Some called this revenant Wooly Booger, and he wreaked out vengeance on anyone entering his family plot. Then fingers pointed to a certain headstone belonging to Willie Boucher because, well, it sounded kind of like Woolly Booger. Certainly, he was the killer. Yet, Willie was only a one year old when he died.

Willie's Grave.

Still, there might have been a boogeyman there. In the spring of 1957, the half-clothed corpse of a young woman was found on a lover's lane road by Big Darby Creek near Darbydale by four teens heading out to fly fish. The murderer had wrapped a towel around the body before stuffing it in a feed sack and dumping it into a puddle of water. Police had a tough time finding out who murdered the girl, and many-a-parent probably warned their children from Columbus, past Darbydale, and beyond that they better be in by dark because there was a boogeyman on the loose near Darbydale. And they were right.

Gallia County

Bethel Cemetery
Bethel Road
Patriot, Ohio 45658
38.797728, -82.460686
38.800119,-82.460632

Dark Entity

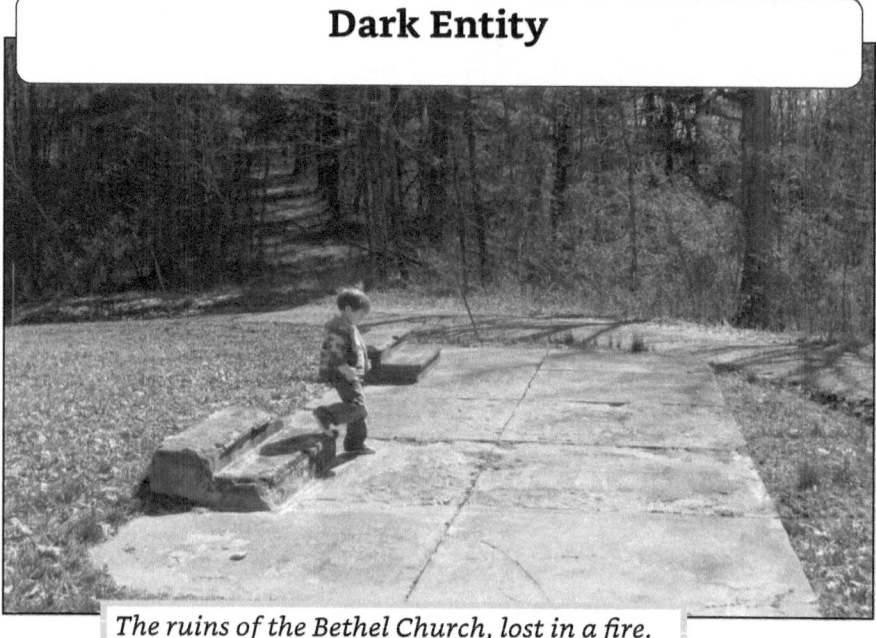

The ruins of the Bethel Church, lost in a fire.

Many, many years ago, a community was built around this area with homes and farms. As times changed, people died away or moved, leaving all but a home or two in the vicinity, and the shell of a long-gone church with its graveyard. For years, people visiting the cemetery have witnessed a tall, dark and cloaked entity wandering down the hillside as if protecting what remains. It appears with fog creeping up from the valley.

Hancock County

Weidler's Pass Railroad
6566 County Road 236
Findlay, Ohio 45840
41.071554,-83.594713

Headless Ghost of Weidler's Pass

Weidler's Pass—where a ghostly lantern weaves and bobs and a headless man walks the tracks.

The small section of tracks that once ran across B. Weidler's property had a short bypass lane to facilitate traffic. It was a passing siding or section of track paralleling the mainline and joined at both ends. An entire train could pull over at this section so another could pass in the opposite direction.

It was during a routine run in the chilly days of November of 1889, Jimmy Welsh, a freight train conductor, was on this section of railway. Just past the intersection of the roadway, he plummeted from a car that had broken away from another. He tumbled to the tracks at a dizzying speed. Within seconds, the wheels of the train that had split into two sections crushed him. He was instantly beheaded.

Only a few short months later, trains running the Lake Erie and Western Railroad between Findlay and Fostoria began seeing a headless apparition carrying a lantern on their midnight run. As the lantern light danced about above the train tracks, it was clear that the ghost was searching for something along the ground in the exact spot the conductor lost his head.

Hartman Cemetery
8702 Township Highway 44
Findlay, Ohio 45840
40.96872, -83.708267

The Unrested Graves

HARTMAN
CEMETERY

Those visiting the cemetery and then returning a week later have noticed upon return that graves are moved. Legends have long been passed down that if you travel to the cemetery and choose a grave, it will be in a different place if you come back in a week.

Mt. Blanchard Cemetery
Carrie Bell's Grave
Co. Hwy 273/4a and
Cemetery Drive
Mt Blanchard, Ohio 45867
40.904408, -83.552259

Do Not Look Back

There is a statue for a young wife named Carrie Bell at Mt Blanchard Cemetery that is haunted. If you place your fingers on her grave, do not turn your back to her when you step away. Those who have touched her stone, turned around, and walked the opposite direction have heard footsteps following them. Others see her eyes glow a deep, vibrant red, and the gaze follows those who stride away.

Henry County

Harris-Jones Cemetery
7250 County Road 7
Napoleon, Ohio 43545
41.396350, -83.99943

Crybaby Hill

Visitors who tarry outside the cemetery hear the sound of babies crying. Then, of course, in autumn, the rustling of tiny hands and feet can be heard as the dead babies crawl across the farm fields and through the corn surrounding the small hillside of the cemetery.

Girty's Island
Napoleon, Ohio 43545
41.32926,-84.155302
You can see it from
Cole Cemetery:
Co Rd Z
Napoleon, Ohio 43545
41.327197,-84.151869

Renegade Ghost

Girty's Island.

In the 1790s, on the north bank of the Maumee River not far from Florida, Ohio, there was a trading post owned by a man named James Girty. The bend where it stood was called Girty's Point. James was a British supporter and supplied local Indians with weapons and trade goods to fight the U.S. military and settlers.

Near the trading post was a forty-acre island that was partly farmed and partly covered in thick brush. James had a brother named Simon who, like James, had been held captive in his early teens by Indians and learned the language and customs of the people. Both would remain loyal to the British and the Indians who had kidnapped them. But while James used his trading post to aid in the war efforts, Simon was a fighter who was horrifically hostile to settlers. James and Simon would hide out on the island when the military passed through between forts in the region. For years, the island has been rumored to be haunted by Simon Girty. For those who dare to go near the island, his ghost will chase them away. If Simon Girty catches them, he will torture them like he tortured the settlers he fought and captured.

North Turkeyfoot Wildlife Area
US-24
McClure, Ohio 43534
41.413683, -83.989495

Lost Gold of Shunk

Near Shunk and in North Turkey Foot Wildlife Area.

In August of 1794, Revolutionary War General Mad Anthony Wayne had already traversed the land from Cincinnati to Toledo. His troops built a wall of forts along the way with his main goals to protect the settlers from Indian attacks and forcibly push Indians out of Ohio. He came face to face with Shawnee, Delaware, Wyandot, and Miami along the Maumee River, where a barrier of fallen timbers had been left behind from a storm.

The battle did not go so well for the Indians. Mad Anthony had three times as many fighters, and the Indians were defeated in a short amount of time and retreated. But in their grasp, they had managed to steal the soldiers' pay in gold sheets. Quickly, they hid the money along a bend in a river now known as Turkeyfoot Creek near the town of Shunk. They planned on returning later to retrieve it. However, they never got the chance.

The legends tell the Indians left the ghost of a dead warrior on the bank of the Turkeyfoot Creek to protect it so no one but those who hid it would ever uncover its secret place. Those who have searched it out have come face to face with the ghost who guards it—a warrior perched high atop a white horse. Long ago, a group of travelers came upon the spirit while crossing the Precht Bridge on horseback. It forced them to turn and go in the opposite direction. Many have dared to challenge the curse; all have failed. There is a price that must be paid for those who come into contact with the ghost, including a young boy in the 1800s. All have fallen victim to shock and loss of memory.

The Precht Bridge before being torn down. The area of the ghostly rider can be seen at Turkeyfoot Wildlife Area. (41.413796, -83.989560)

The Precht Bridge, now gone, was named for William Precht, who died there in a tractor accident. Occasionally, witnesses hiking the trails at North Turkeyfoot Wildlife Area report seeing his ghost coming up the bank of the creek.

North Turkeyfoot Creek and the old bridge before it was demolished.

Highland County

Fallsville Wildlife Area
10211 Careytown Road
New Vienna, Ohio 45159
Parking:
39.285561, -83.630011
Old Homestead:
39.286057, -83.632949

Christmas Ghost

Fallsville.

Fallsville. Where a town once thrived. Now only a ghost remains.

One chilly Christmas Eve in the 1880s, two sisters living alone in an isolated pocket of Highland County heard a rap-rap upon their door. Few people were remaining in the tiny town that once surrounded their home. And especially on a wintery Christmas night, they would not know who would dare to brave the weather and visit. Startled, they arose to part the curtains and peered out the window into the snowy night.

Beneath a moon and at the end of their walkway, there stood an Indian in full dress. Intrigued, and with wide eyes, they watched his mouth moving as if trying to form words. His fingers were weaving in sign language. But unable to hear his words nor understand the sign language, they did not know what he wanted from them. Before the two could decide to open the door or not, he simply vanished. This mysterious apparition came each Christmas after that. The two women hired an interpreter to read the hand signs, and from that deciphering, they found that there was tribal treasure buried on the property, and he had come to claim it.

The story would travel around the community, and the sisters were easy prey for gossip. Many knew the women well. The two sisters were the daughters of Simon and Elizabeth Clouser, who bought and settled on a couple of parcels of land along the waterfalls of Clear Creek many years earlier. The property came with an 1812 two-story stone home initially built by a John Timberlake, who had recorded the town around him as Fallsville in 1848.

Its industry was a grist mill built by the waterfall with Simon's hands. There was a church, a cemetery, and five small blocks of streets with about eight homes across the creek. Hoping to gain status as the county seat, the town hardly grew above six families, one of them Simon's own with three children: Susanna, Charlotte, and Lewis. Although Lewis would eventually move away to New York and the parents would pass away at ripe old ages, the two Clouser sisters lived out their days quietly in the home and were among the last citizens of the community.

The Christmas ghost story lent credence to more rumors surrounding the two. Some said they clung to old superstitions, greeting strangers visiting the falls along Clear Creek. As the visitors walked away, the sisters threw salt at their feet to protect the town from evil.

Little remains of Fallsville except for a mark on the map, some steps slightly visible by the falls, and the Methodist Church and cemetery. The house was torn down around the 1970s, but a bit of the old Clouser home where the Indian visited remains. The ghost of the Indian still visits the wildlife area. Hikers hear music in the tiny woodlots and meadows, and the jingling of a bell makes an eerie beckoning call to the curious, luring them away from the treasure. And on some evenings before Christmas Day, he is seen standing on the path in front of the heap of the old home still trying to claim his tribal treasures.

Standing where the ghost once stood on Christmas Eve. The pile of bricks and stone is pretty much all remaining of the home.

You can visit the remains of the Clouser homestead at Fallsville Wildlife Area, park in the small lot, and walk the roadway back. It is a beautiful hike and not scary at all. If you walk the short dirt road and stop at the open area and look to the left, you can see where the Clouser home used to be and perhaps see the ghost.

Hocking County

Hocking Hills State Park
Old Man's Cave
19852 OH-664
Logan, Ohio 43138
39.435351, -82.541179

The Legend of Old Man's Cave

Old Man's Cave (also once known as Dead Man's Cave): Old Man's Cave is a popular tourist attraction in southeastern Ohio featuring a hiking trail that winds through a long, tree-lined gorge with cliff edges, waterfalls, and unique rock formations.

There once was a quiet town between Logan and South Bloomingville called Cedar Grove. It was settled near a sandstone gorge with a meandering stream called Cedar Creek that ran beneath tall cliffs. These cliff walls were covered with recess caves of all shapes and sizes, with one standing out as the largest and called Old Man's Cave.

Just as people like to hike the gorge today, in the early 1900s, it was not uncommon for sightseers to walk the paths beneath the huge hemlocks and view the waterfalls. Back then, though and illegal today, when the area was privately owned, much wilder, and fewer people visited, it was also common for locals to set up ropes on the cliff walls and swing across the wide expanse of the creek below. It was much to the delight and awe of the tourists traveling on the trail beneath.

Old Man's Cave about the time of the story.

One afternoon, two young men by the names of Kreig and Hillis had set up a rope near Old Man's Cave, descending until they were about 50 feet from the creek water. They took turns swinging, basking in the applause from onlookers until Kreig saw a peculiar old man with white hair, gray beard, and wearing old-fashioned leather clothing strolling along the trail. He carried an ancient rifle on his right shoulder, and by his side, a large hound kept stride. Kreig pointed it out to Hillis, who was descending the rope. As Hillis began to swing, the old man stopped and seemed as absorbed in the antics as those milling around the creek.

After a while, the old man appeared to lose interest. He continued up the trail and into the cave, and as he reached the entrance, he passed a young couple seated on a rock engaged in pleasant conversation. Kreig was still watching with great fascination when he saw the couple turn their heads toward the man as if they had just noticed him. With that, the girl threw her palms to her lips and fell in a faint! Suddenly, those below were either in an uproar, appearing frightened and scurrying around or staring in awe at the old man. Kreig's eyes went from the scene below and then to the old man who had slipped into the large recess cave. Then unexpectedly, the old man and his dog sunk into the sand at the bottom, vanishing.

There was a certain mystery as to where this old ghost originated. From the testimonies of those hailing from the town of Cedar Grove, the old man was discovered many years ago by two young boys who lived in the town and were exploring the valley and its many nooks and crannies. Growing bored after climbing one boulder after another, they built a small fire within a large recess cave that overlooked a valley of hemlocks and craggy rocks.

One of the boys, the younger of the two, was uncertain about visiting this particular cave. It was rumored to be haunted. Some had heard the low baying of a hound at night there, but when they searched for the dog, it could never be found. The boys had only been inside the cave a few minutes when the crunch of footsteps on leaves and sand forced them to look up from the flames. An old man and a large, white dog, staying close to the man's side, walked past them. The man had a long, gray beard, old-fashioned clothing, and leather moccasins. He carried an antique rifle over his shoulder. The man appeared to be interested in the back of the cave. He paced back and forth near the edge of the far rocks and, upon coming to a standstill, peered intently at a shallow depression in the sandstone earth.

Then both the man and the dog vanished into the depression as if they had not been there at all!

Eagerly, the boys sought help from some local adults at Cedar Grove, investigating the place the old man had disappeared. With mattocks and shovels, a small crew of men removed rocks and dug out the hollow in the cave's sandstone floor. They exposed two sets of bones—a man and a dog, an old flintlock rifle with the date of 1702 etched into the wood, and some cooking pots. There was also a scratching in the stone that stated the man's name as Retzler and the date of death as 1777.

For a long time, many travelers would come to visit to see the remains inside the cave they dubbed Retzler's Cave, Dead Man's Cave, or Old Man's Cave. They would stare down at the old bones and wonder who the man and dog had once been. Some would hear the baying of a hound dog far away, and rumors prevailed that the ghostly dog returned, but for what reason, they did not know. After a while, the bones disappeared. The curious stopped coming, and the story faded away except for a few living in the community who brought it up once in a while when lingering outside the grocery store.

One late autumn night not too long ago, a park ranger listened intently to the sound of a dog howling deep in the gorge. Occasionally, dogs from the scattering of homes nearby strayed from their backyards. They usually found their way home, but this particular dog sounded like a hunting hound, and the frantic bay most certainly meant it had treed a raccoon. It could mean that poachers were hunting in the park. The ranger snatched up his flashlight and worked his way down the rugged trail and into the gorge. He followed the sound of the dog, filtering out the splash of a waterfall and the crunch of sandstone at his feet.

But even while he got closer to the hound's yowling howls and threw the beam of his flashlight upward, he could see little in the fog flowing up along the rock cliff. He saw no dog in the darkness. And yet, the howls got louder and louder until they seemed to be circling him just out of reach. He whipped his flashlight around in a circle, then just as suddenly as the dog's baying came, it ceased.

For years, many have heard the baying of a phantom dog within the gorge and cave area called Old Man's Cave. Its presence is explained like this—

Before the settling of the towns of Logan and Cedar Grove, some trappers lived along Cedar Creek, a stream that worked its way through a deep sandstone gorge. These men made their home in modest one-room cabins or animal-skin tents abutting the small caves within the valley. They made a living selling the pelts of the many fur-bearing creatures like otter and fox that roamed the region at the time.

As their jobs required them to travel far into the wilderness, they were gone for many days at a time. One winter, upon returning from a seasonal hunt, neighbors noticed that one particular trapper named Retzler, who made his home in a cave outcropping along with his dog Harper had not been seen in quite some time. The usually heavily-traveled path to his abode was overgrown, and there was no sign of his faithful hound who bayed whenever someone neared the camp.

After taking the footpath that led to the cave, they lifted the flap of his leather-hide tent and peered inside. Before them lay the dead trapper along with his old hound dog dead by his side. They carefully lifted the limp bodies of the man and dog and placed them in a shallow hole they had dug in the back of the cave and covered them with sand.

Hocking Hills State Park
Ash Cave
OH-56
South Bloomingville, Ohio 43152
39.395993,-82.545927

Pale Lady

Naturalist Pat Quackenbush leading a hike in Ash Cave. I think a spirit in the cave must be fond of him. One time, while I was on a night hike as a volunteer, I was assigned to be the last hiker to make sure no one was left behind. A good friend of Pat's, Gary Bergstrand, hiked the end with me and we struck up a quiet conversation just before Pat ended his talk at this location. I heard a loud "SHHH!" Thinking that it was my imagination, I turned to Gary and asked him if he heard the odd sound. He chuckled and said, "Yep, I think we just got shushed by a ghost!"

Hikers have seen the ghost of a young woman dressed in 1920s clothing along the trail that winds its way to the Ash Cave waterfall. She peers from behind trees and tags along on guided night hikes, easing back just far enough to appear like one of the group until she fades away.

***Ash Cave** –Where a ghostly lady has been seen along the trail.*

On one particular night hike, park naturalist Pat Quackenbush noted a straggler in his group of hikers. As was customary on the walks he led, Pat would stop six or seven times along the trail, pointing out plants and wildlife. Pat had been a naturalist for well over 40 years; he knew the tricks of the trade. He learned early on to make a routine of silently taking a headcount of those in the group when he stopped to make sure nobody had gotten left behind in the dark. As Pat paused at a beech tree for his seventh and final stop, he began to count out his twelve hikers. With a flush of uncertainty, he realized there were thirteen—somehow, he miscalculated the last six times, or someone had joined the group. He also noted that this thirteenth hiker was deathly pale and dressed in a feed sack dress common in the 1920s.

Pat swallowed hard, then turned to the group. He may have been a naturalist a long time, but he would do something he had never done before on a hike—he asked the hikers before him if they could see a mysterious shadow in the rear of the group. Each turned with uncertainty, and some gasped. With that, the shadow took a couple of steps and vanished. Everyone in the group saw the ghost!

Wayne National Forest
Tinker's Cave
12318 Burton Hill Road
New Straitsville, Ohio 43766
39.546255, -82.226422
(Watch for the gravel pull-off. The rugged trail is
on the same side as the pull-off.)

Legend of the Dead Horse Thief

Horse Thief Cave/Tinker's Cave.

A man and horses haunt an ancient rock shelter off a lonely stretch of dirt-gravel road at the head of a deep valley. He died many years ago and the reason for this haunting might have something to do with the dead man's dirty deeds in life—

It was late one afternoon in the mid-1800s when a lone farmer herded his goats into the back yard of the Buntz House hostel in Logan. The farmer told the inn owner that he had come to town to sell a herd of his goats. He needed a place to stay for the night, but he could not afford the full night's stay up front. He assured the hostel owner that he would pay half now and the rest in the morning and after he sold the goats. As an act of goodwill, he also suggested that the owner could lock the gates with the goats inside his yard as insurance he would not leave without paying.

The farmer was quite charming and convincing, so the owner agreed to the arrangement, received half the payment, and locked the goats inside the yard. The next morning, however, the goats and farmer had vanished without paying what was due. Only several wooden planks lying askew in the backyard threw light on how the thief had made his escape—he had placed boards up and over the wooden fence so the goats could clamber over in the dark of night, and he could steal away without unlocking the gates.

The farmer was not a farmer at all, but a well-known thief named Shep Tinker who had stolen someone's goats and needed a place to hide for the night while he fled.

Old newspapers would often recall Shep Tinker swindled business owners and terrorized farmers by stealing their animals all over nearby counties where his well-to-do family had their farm. He hid the livestock in the many caves of the region until he could move them to northern Ohio to sell there.

Many stories were told of his exploits, and it was rumored Shepherd Tinker helped Confederate soldiers, led by John Morgan, during their raids through Ohio by giving his men horses stolen from the town of Logan. He spent time in prison off and on. Once, he even charmed a girl, whose job was to bring food to the prisoners, into helping him escape by stealing the warden's keys.

Another time, he stole a completely black horse belonging to Doctor James Dew. Doctor Dew, upon seeing Shep Tinker sneak off with his horse, took off after Tinker. As darkness came, Doctor Dew had nearly caught up with Tinker, but realizing he was about to be overtaken, Tinker bound the muzzle of the horse with a white cloth and turned the horse around until he was heading toward Doctor Dew. In the darkness, Doctor Dew called out to Tinker and asked if the man had seen a rider with a black horse. Tinker said, "Yes, I did! He went thataway!" He pointed Doctor Dew in the direction he had come. The doctor took off again after his stolen horse, not realizing until later he had been tricked by the horse thief!

Shepherd Tinker disappeared after the Civil War. Locals always said that Shep stole horses from the wrong farmer and ended up on the short end of a noose right in the very cave where he hid most of his stolen animals and the large rock shelter that bears his name, Tinker's Cave.

It also holds his ghost and the ghosts of the horses he had stolen. Hikers have heard muffled whinnies and shuffles of hooves inside the cave and the mumbles of Shep boasting about the thousands of horses he stole.

Jackson County

Salem Church Cemetery
Route 124 and Salem Road
Wellston, Ohio 45692
39.078658, -82.501895

The Knock-Knock Back

Salem Church—knock-knock and it might knock-knock back.

The Salem Cemetery is the site of the monument honoring the unknown Confederates killed during a Civil War battle nearby when General John Morgan made his infamous raid through Ohio in July of 1863. Several of Morgan's men were killed when they crossed paths with Ohio militia on the hillsides of nearby Berlin Crossroads. Between 4 and 12 were killed, have been buried nearby, and may haunt the cemetery. The church is home to the Knock-Knock Ghost. If you knock-knock gently on the door, you may hear someone—or *something* knock-knock back.

Salem Road
Berlin Crossroads, Ohio 45692
39.080316, -82.518896

Lost on Earth

Berlin Crossroads.

Berlin Crossroads, just outside Jackson, was initially a small community settled by African Americans and freed persons of color. During the mid-1800s, the area became an important stopping point along a certain route for fugitive slaves escaping to freedom from Virginia and Kentucky. Some came by horse and others by foot mostly to a farm owned by Noah Nooks, a free person of color, who secreted them safely off to others in Wilkesville, Albany, and Athens.

In the early years, people riding their buggies past Old Baptist Cemetery on Salem Cemetery Road would see a woman in a long white robe walking beside their carriage, keeping pace with the horse. Many knew that those in Berlin Crossroads opened their homes to escaping slaves, but most outsiders kept to their business and said nothing about the comings and goings of those in the community. When passersby saw the woman, they assumed by her quickened steps she was heading toward the town and its safety. But as they passed and looked down, she appeared unaware of those staring down at her. Her face was faded like a corpse, and they grasped she was long-dead. Nobody knows how the mysterious woman died. They believed, however, that she is forever heading toward freedom but is bound to walk the earth, unable to get to her destination.

Lake County

Fairport Harbor Lighthouse
129 Second Street
Fairport Harbor, Ohio 44077
41.757451,-81.277782

Haunted Lighthouse

Lake County's Fairport Harbor Lighthouse has served as a beacon of safety for many. Not only was it a safe harbor for ships traveling along the shoreline, it provided sanctuary for slaves heading to Canada. It is also home to a ghost. In 1871, when Captain Joseph Babcock came to be head keeper of the lighthouse, his wife and family kept several cats in the living quarters which is now the museum.

For years, volunteers and curators at the museum have seen what they described as a ghostly cat playing in the rooms. During the installation of a new air conditioning system, the mummified remains of a cat was discovered between the walls, probably one of the cats from the Babcock family stay there—and the reason for the ghostly presence.

Licking County

Buxton Inn
313 E Broadway Street
Granville, Ohio 43023
40.067776,-82.516551

A Haunting at Buxton

A ghost from its early days as a guesthouse haunts the Buxton Inn. She walks along the hallway and tarries near Room 9, even talking to visitors on occasion. Some believe it is Bonnie Bounell, a previous owner who died in the room.

Cedar Hill Cemetery
275 N Cedar Street
Newark, Ohio 43055
40.06996,-82.388148

A Screaming Tomb and Roaming Baby Eyes

Visiting the Baker Mausoleum. While my son knocked and I listened, the monument of a woman to our left seemed to be watching, bored and impatient, as if she has seen more than us doing this.

Cedar Hill Cemetery has some unusual ghosts like the Woman in White who strolls among the graves. The large Baker Mausoleum has a life-size weeping angel guarding those within and a dark, rusted door barring anyone wanting to steal inside. Some who knock gently on the door and push an ear up against the gritty metal have heard screams from within the stone walls.

Then there is Roaming Baby Eyes—a gravestone with a baby's face carved into the stone not far from the Baker Mausoleum. If you stare at the baby's face while counting to sixty, then turn your head away and look at it again, the baby's head will turn just slightly too!

The Licking County Historic Jail
46 S 3rd Street
Newark, Ohio 43055
40.056171, -82.401398

Ghosts of Serial Killers, Murderers, Insane, and a Sweet Kid from Kentucky Lynched by a Ruthless Mob

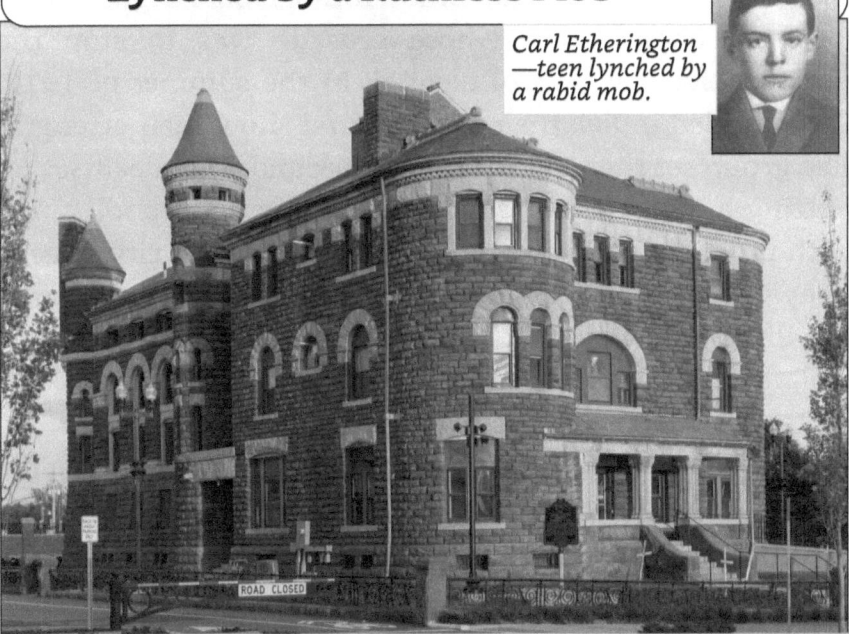

Carl Etherington —teen lynched by a rabid mob.

The Licking County Jail. The front three levels housed the sheriff's family and a jail matron. The rear held 32 jail cells, each 8' x 8' in size.
Image: Library of Congress

What could possibly go wrong when marshals confront a bunch of drunk thugs while raiding their saloon in the name of Prohibition? Well, a murder followed by a ghost for starters—

Built in 1889, the Licking County Jail has housed serial killers, murderers, and the insane. For example, on January 6th, 1947, Missus Laura Belle Devlin, dubbed the Handsaw Slayer stayed there. She murdered and then dismembered her 72-year-old husband's corpse with a sickle and saw, then tossed the remains into their coal stove to dispose of the evidence. There were at least 22 deaths within those walls, seven of those being suicides. Four of the deaths were sheriffs who died from heart attacks. And there was one informal lynching—

Conservative religious factions had revived the Prohibition Movement in the early 1900s. By 1910, it was in full swing as were more than 80 saloons and 30 brothels in the city of Newark. The Ohio Anti-Saloon League was a lobbying organization whose crusade was to stop the consumption and sale of alcohol. In the summer of 1910, they decided to flex their muscles and show their strength. The group set their sights on Newark and were dead-set on putting a stop to the scandalous selling of alcohol, along with prostitution and gambling right along the city streets. They were not only tired of the local police's inability to stop the illicit behavior, but also turning a blind eye to liquor violations. They knew Sheriff William Linke was taking protection money from bars which he would not close.

League President Wayne Wheeler hired a few private detectives from Cleveland and had them deputized before the upcoming raid at 8:30 a.m. July 8th. Next, the men set out to sweep several local saloons and arrest the owners. The raids did not fare well. One group of marshals was trapped in a bar by a mob of angry drunks and had to flee out the back door. One marshal, 17-year-old Carl Etherington red-headed and hailing from Kentucky, made a desperate run from the ruffians, jumping on to the interurban streetcar.

He was able to ride for a couple of miles only to be stopped by 41-year-old William Howard. An ex-Newark cop, Howard was now proprietor of the Last Chance Saloon. He began beating Etherington with a blackjack until the teenager fell to the blows. But as Etherington went to the ground, he drew his revolver and shot Howard in the stomach. Almost instantly, a crowd came upon Etherington and beat him severely, then dragged him to a cell at the Licking County Jail.

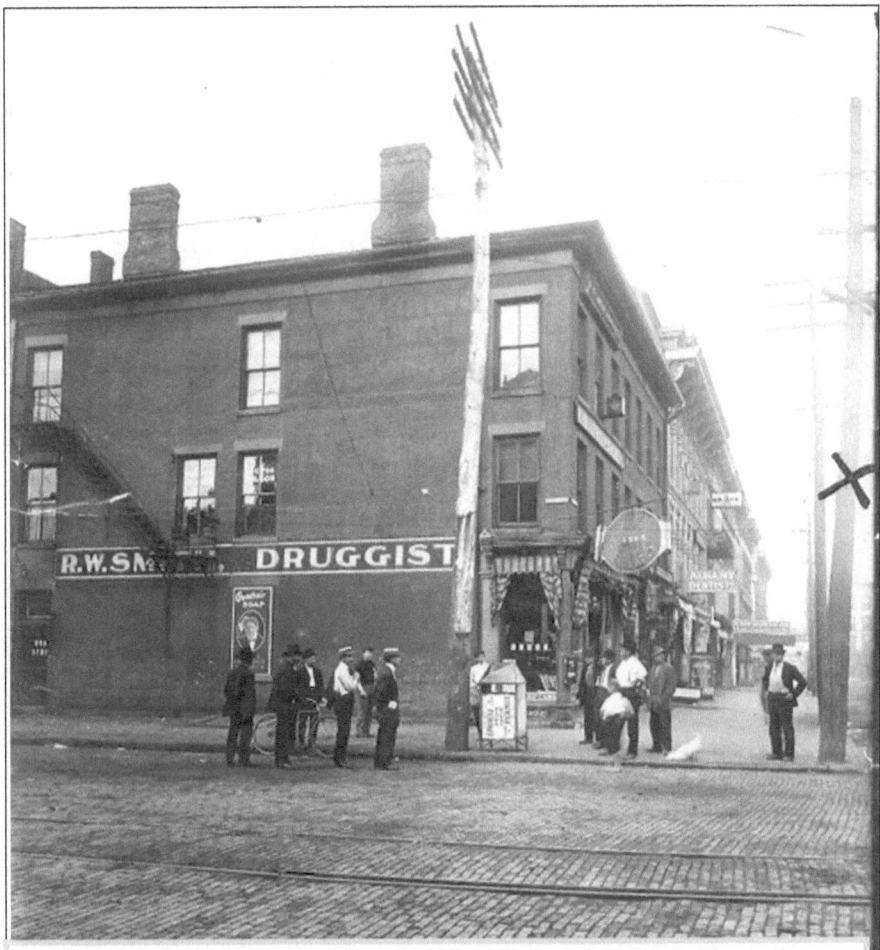

Etherington was hanged on July 8th, 1910 from this pole on the southeast corner of the courthouse square—intersection at the corner of South Park Place and 2nd Streets.
39 S Park Place Newark, Ohio 43055 (40.057460, -82.400626)
Image: Newark Advocate and Licking County Historical Society

When word came that evening that Howard had died, at 10:30 p.m., a mob tore up the railroad tracks for a tie and violently bashed the cell door in. Even as the horrified teen listened to the sound of the door crashing outside, he was more concerned about his mother as he sobbed to the guard: "What will mother say when she hears of this?"

They proceeded to beat him again savagely and some say until he died in that cell. But it was not enough. They whisked the teen outside and hanged him from a telegraph pole while thousands, including children, watched. The macabre lynching would end in 20 to 25 first-degree murder indictments, removal of the county sheriff, and the resignation of the mayor.

It also may have left behind ghosts from its violent past. Doors slam. Cries of help ring out, and footsteps pad along the floors. Shadowy figures walk the hallways, and there is an occasional jingle of keys. But why not find out about its ghostly past yourself? You might run into poor Carl Etherington or part of his crazed lynching mob, or even the Handsaw Slayer, herself. The Licking County Governmental Preservation Society oversees the Licking County Historic Jail. They offer both historical and paranormal tours.

Lorain County

**Ruins of Swift Mansion -
Light and Hope Orphanage**
*52374 Gore Orphanage Road
Amherst, Ohio 44001
41.355052, -82.335234*

Gore Orphanage

The Swift Mansion—part of Light and Hope Orphanage aka "Gore Orphanage" before it burned down.

There's a story about an orphanage in Lorain County. While the children who lived there were sleeping in their beds, Old Man Gore, who ran the place, nailed all their doors shut. Then, he lit a match, caught the place on fire. Inside, the children awakened to a fiery death, tiny fists pounding on the barred windows and doors. Then they all went up in flames.

Well, not exactly. There was an orphanage on this little piece of land along Gore Road (named for the triangular shape) built from the Johnathon Swift Mansion and a few surrounding farms. It would become the home of the Wilber family for about thirty-five years. Later, it caught the eye of John Sprunger, wealthy industrialist/builder, and his wife, Katie.

Right: Light and Hope Orphanage — Girls' quarters—

Left: Light and Hope Orphanage — Boys' quarters—

A capitalist at heart, Sprunger had founded the Light and Hope Missionary Society in 1893 along with the Light and Hope Orphanage. Around 1903, Sprunger had purchased the Hughes farm in Amherst along with three other neighboring farms, including the Howard's farm and buildings to house the children.

It was here the Sprungers established the printing shop and publishing company under the guise of an orphanage trade training center for children. Actually, the children, ranging from about seven to seventeen, were indentured servants—forced to do free work providing services in the printing company and working the farm. Sprunger also rented the children out for agricultural work as hired hands to surrounding farms.

His scheme was not new—children had been bought from Victorian workhouses and overworked without wages in exchange for board and food as pauper apprentices in England since the 17th century. To the public eye, he posed as a saint; his undertakings had all the appearances of a training facility where teachers taught boys a trade and girls learned domestic sciences. In reality, the children were victims of Sprunger's capitalist greed with the deceptive outward appearance of evangelism and charity.

The boys lived at the Hughes farm, and the girls dwelt at the old Howard farm. The children's overseers lived at the Swift Mansion. Light and Hope Orphanage eventually encompassed over 500 acres. A 1910 U.S. census shows forty-five people were living on the property, including twenty-seven children, Katie and John Sprunger, and fifteen helpers and assistants. In actuality, sources state there could have been up to 125 children on the property at a single time. The caretakers were not caregivers at all, but wardens/overseers for the laboring children. Sprunger treated children like slaves and got rich off their labors.

From the onset, the complaints and investigations of abuse and slave labor at the farms plagued the orphanage. It came to a head in 1909 when children began to run away and tell local, empathetic Amherst townspeople about their abuse. It got so bad that nearby townspeople established an underground railroad for escaping children.

Beatings were a common form of punishment to the children by both overseers, the Sprungers, and local farmers when they worked. The Sprungers also forced their slave labor to eat spoiled food. Bedbugs, lice, and rats were commonplace in their cots at night. A sick cow found dead in a field was used for the children's meals. Instead of a doctor's care and medicines, they called upon prayer for healing. A litter of bunnies was strangled in front of the children by a teacher to threaten the boys and girls. The orphanage, by judge ruling, was placed into different hands.

With a little bit of searching, you can still find this horse hitching post.

The Swift Mansion—

So it was true that a cruel, horrible man ran the orphanage. And there was also a fire during the time that authorities investigated the orphanage over allegations of abuse—in 1910, a boxcar filled with oil and printing supplies burned. It was a three-story building completely destroyed used for the printing of the Sprunger's Light and Hope Magazine. It exploded so heartily that flames filled the sky. There is no mention in newspapers of children killed during the explosion or fire, nor is there mention that there was an investigation by local authorities held to check for foul play or deaths. Records of the number of children at the orphanage were poorly kept and rarely accurate.

That said, although the considerable fire that killed hundreds of children may not be confirmed, there are ghosts of its past and plenty of them. The orphanage stayed open until 1916. The old mansion was burned down in 1923 by some homeless taking up residence. People did die here—two of the initial owners, the Swift children, are buried in the Gore Orphanage/Andress family cemetery. There are probably a few settlers who died here even earlier than them. At least one little orphan boy was killed nearby, 'coasting' on the back of a car. And those old, disturbing memories still linger of cruelty on the property to sad little orphans who may have returned to the place to haunt Old Man Sprunger and his hired hands for their beatings and slavery.

There have been tales of a ghost child swinging on an old tree. And while carrying a recorder at Gore Orphanage, I heard a child's voice say softly "Tryphenia"—that is how I found out about the Swift's children, researching what the word meant and finding it was the name of a daughter who died at age five in 1831 there.

It is worth the hike beneath the trees to search out the foundation, find the old well, imagine what it looked like before fire burned the mansion to the ground. Some put baby powder on the back of their car to see the tiny handprints show up. Try it. Maybe, you'll see the ghost of someone's past like thousands before you. Because they say, they have.

Just past the ruins of Swift Mansion, a bridge crosses the Vermilion River. This span is near the location of the actual orphanage buildings—cottages for girls and boys. Some see mists and lights at the bridge. Those who park their cars in the gravel pull-off before the bridge and turn off their vehicles have gotten small, dusty handprints on their car windows and windshield. And the sound of children crying can be heard when driving away.

Dean's Bridge
9604 Dean Road
(Twp Hwy 66)
Wakeman, Ohio 44889
41.348786,-82.344897

The Cursed Noose

A man hung himself on the bridge in the late 1800s. When those who found his body took him down, they left the noosed rope. It was there for a long time, rotted away, then fell into the river below and was swept downstream. After the hanging, some travelers crossing the bridge would see the ghostly rope hanging from the girders, swinging back and forth. Anyone who saw it died not long after. They tried to close the road down, but occasionally folks still drive through it.

Lucas County

Columbian House
3 N River Road
Waterville, Ohio 43566
41.499273, -83.71735

Return of the Drunken Old Man

In the early 1800s, John Pray built a three-story stagecoach inn and meeting house along the Maumee River. As the years passed, there would be a dressmaker's shop, church, small businesses, school, drugstore, and doctor's office within its walls. There was even a place for the town's jail on one floor, used to house prisoners on their way to Maumee, the town seat.

A strange incident occurred in its early years. An old man, the local drunk, was locked in the jail one night to sleep off his liquor. While he was there, he knocked and banged on the walls, complaining that he was sick. In the morning, when the local jailkeeper opened the door to release his prisoner, the old man was stone cold dead. After that, those staying in certain parts of the Columbian House would hear ghostly banging on the walls from time to time.

Gibbs Road Bridge
Township Highway 77
Sylvania, Ohio 43560
41.717448,-83.801901

The Peculiar Haunt on Gibbs Road Bridge

Some say it is dangerous to go out to the cement-walled Gibbs Road Bridge just off Sylvania-Metamora Road. For years, ghost seekers have followed the roads from outlying areas and stopped just short of the bridge. They have reported seeing lights coming toward them and have seen the hazy remains of someone walking along the road. The peculiar events are supposed leftover from the numerous deadly traffic accidents and a suicide there.

Ravine Cemetery
6455 Ravine Drive
Sylvania, Ohio 43560
41.71035,-83.698645

The Unresolved Wife

At Ravine Cemetery, there is a lonely grave and a haunt. A woman married three times, and each time she outlived her husband. With each husband, she had many children. When she died, the children fought over which father she would be buried beside. Unable to agree, they buried her alone and away from all the husbands. Soon after her burial, passersby began seeing the woman's ghost wandering frantically from one husband's grave to the next, eternally accounting for each of them and unresolved, unable to choose just one herself.

Secor Metropark
Wolfinger Cemetery
9900 Wolfinger Road
Holland, Ohio 43528
41.666592, -83.785296

Three Little Ghosts

A ghostly child in long, white grave clothes peers at me with arms resting on the fence at the cemetery.

The pioneers who settled in the early 1800s near Sylvania included farmer Jacob Wolfinger who built a homestead where Secor Park is today. The burials of two of his children on his farm would be the beginnings of Wolfinger cemetery. As the community grew, so did the cemetery. Epidemics would take their toll, including the Gowman children—6-year-old Earnest, 8-year-old Thomas, and 10-year-old Rebeca, who died within weeks of each other in December 1865 and January 1866. Some believe these three haunt the cemetery—watching, laughing, and playing.

Marion County

Harding Home
Presidential Site
380 Mt Vernon Avenue
Marion, Ohio 43302
40.586476, -83.121494

Home of the Dead President

Most haunted homes get stuck with old, angry relatives banging on the walls or the booms and rattles of some ne'er-do-well who cut their life short with a sturdy rafter, noosed rope, and rickety chair. Not so with the Harding Home in Marion. Instead, the ghost of President Harding haunts it. Warren G. Harding and his wife lived here from 1891 to 1915 before his presidency, and it still has a ghost clock in the library that stopped working the moment he died from a heart attack in 1923.

St Mary's Cemetery
Inie Driffhein Grave
763 Delaware Avenue
Marion, Ohio 43302
40.5755,-83.125062

Gypsy Queen

Leaving a token at Queen Cleo's Grave.

In March of 1905, a band of gypsies was camping on the farm of Horace W. Riley near Meeker. During this time, a young woman gave birth to a child. Only five days later, the young mother died.

Her name was Inie Driffhein, but Queen Cleo was her stage name as an Algerian street performer in the World's Fair. They buried her in the non-Catholic section of St Mary's Cemetery, but before the woman was laid beneath the ground, the undertakers of Hess and Kirkendall placed her casket in the window so everyone in town could see her.

A cross was placed at her gravesite and later, a stone was also added. Pennies are left at her grave and if you desecrate her grave, you will have bad luck. If you walk the Catholic Cemetery to see her grave, make sure you bring a small gift to leave with Queen Cleo for luck.

**Marion Cemetery
Merchant Ball**
*620 Delaware Avenue
Marion, Ohio 43302
40.577977,-83.120202*

The Mysterious Merchant Ball

The mysterious Merchant Ball.

There are probably logical reasons why the 5,200-pound polished granite ball called the Merchant Ball in Marion Cemetery moves. It only changes position a couple of inches a year, but people have been watching it for well over a hundred years since it was erected in 1896. The reason for its slow progression is a mystery.

One theory of its movement is the Coriolis Effect having to do with the earth's rotation. There is also a thermal expansion and contraction theory suggesting the movement is caused by water freezing and then thawing in the space where the ball contacts the monument's base. But it is a grave, and it is in a cemetery and marking the place of a dead person—Charles Merchant. So there is one other option too. Scientifically speaking, it could be a ghost's energy nudging it a bit. Regardless, the mystery is out there, just waiting for some natural or supernatural explanation. Maybe someday, someone will come up with a scientific reason, or for all the paranormal enthusiasts, get a picture of the ghost of Mister Merchant with a big grin on his ghostly face, sneaking out to shift the ball just a little each night.

Marion Country Club
2415 Crissinger Road
Marion, Ohio 43302
40.542064,-83.155457

She Still Walks

The ghost of a young woman wanders around the Marion Country Club. The reason she sticks around after death is explained like this—Nineteen-year-old Annette Huddle of Harpster worked as a secretary at the country club around 1981. One day, a person walking by found her floating in the Olentangy River near Roberts Road. Everybody knew it was Paul Mack, her boss, that killed her. However, police could not gather enough evidence. He was eventually caught and jailed for murdering another woman in California. And she still walks.

Muskingum County

Moxahala Cemetery
700-798 Moxahala Avenue
Zanesville, Ohio 43701
39.927099,-82.005111

Ghouls of Zanesville

Moxahala Cemetery.

In the winter of 1823, a pretty and popular young woman known as Miss Arnold died from a lingering illness. Her family buried her in the Moxahala Cemetery on the outskirts of town, erected a humble marker over her grave, and tried to forget their sorrow. She was not in the ground long before Jake, the stableman caring for the horses of a Doctor Conant in town, uncovered a tiny pair of pale feet protruding from a stack of hay as he tugged out a pitchfork of hay he was using to freshen stall bedding.

Jake let out a yell, catching the attention of one of the four medical students that Doctor Conant had taken under his wing to teach the tools of his profession. The stableman was swiftly hushed and threatened with all sorts of violence should he speak of what he found. He was sent away for the rest of the day, then while Jake slept a fitful sleep that night, the medical students crept into the barn and secreted the body away.

The old stableman could not stay quiet for long and told the authorities what he had found. The students had stolen the corpse of a virtuous young woman, laid their dirty hands upon her dead flesh to dissect. Ghouls, they called graverobbers in those days, and a mob was formed to find the fiends. They made haste to the cemetery and found a grave laid open, that of poor Miss Arnold. Then they rounded up the students and Doctor Conant, who denied any such wrongdoing. And it appeared, upon attempting to continue detaining the young men, there was no law there making grave robbery a crime! As not to release them to an angry mob, the authorities arrested the students for stealing graveclothes and eventually threw the case out of court. The family never recovered Miss Arnold's dead body. That is the reason she is still around in ghostly form—bystanders see her roaming the cemetery, searching for her missing corpse.

Do not worry about old Doc Conant getting his due. The June 11, 1944 Sunday Times-Signal of Zanesville stated his soul would get no rest either. After death, Conant's grave had been opened many times so the curious could peer inside the stone vault and see his rotting bones.

The Y-Bridge
W Main Street
Zanesville, Ohio 43701
39.940426,-82.014252

Doctor Fowler's Last Ride

The Y-Bridge in the 1960s. Courtesy: Library of Congress.

Early on in Zanesville, bangs, booms, and rattling of windows near the Y-Bridge over the Muskingum were the cause of great alarm by many who thought it was a horde of ghosts creeping up from the depths of the river during certain times. Later, those ghosts were laid to rest when a geologist discovered it was the privately-owned Licking Dam that supplied water power for Isaac Dillon's flour mill causing the spirited activity.

The old dam that offered up ghosts.

The booms and bangs may have stopped when that particular dam ceased to be, but not all the noises went away. Twenty-one-year-old Doctor Isaac Fowler came to Zanesville from Vermont in 1814 and was well-liked in the community during the short time he was there. Only a year into his medical practice in Zanesville, he was crossing the Y-Bridge from the west when the Muskingum River had flooded. At the time, the bridge was lower than in later years, and a strong surge of water was flowing over it. His horse refused to cross at first, but he urged it forward, underestimating the depth and current. Both drowned.

His headstone can be found at the Moxahala Cemetery, although it is unreadable. Into the 1960s, part of his epitaph could still be seen: "—attempting to cross the Muskingum and Licking Bridge. . .was drowned on March 31, 1815, aged 22." After he died, some saw him in ghostly form crossing the bridge before he vanished at the spot he went over. Occasionally, when the water is high, passersby can still hear the cries of his horse and his desperate plea for help.

Stone Academy
115 Jefferson Street
Zanesville, Ohio 43701
39.931492, -82.00588

He Comes Back

The Stone Academy served many purposes, a school, public building, then private residence in 1840. In the 1830's it was the center of abolitionist activity in Putnam; the Ohio Anti-Slavery Society held state conventions in the building in 1835 and 1839. The building also served as part of the Underground Railroad. During this time, an old man escaping slavery hid here, and he died. So as not to call attention to the purpose of his visit, he was buried secretly nearby. Not long after, housewives performing their typical jaunts to town would be startled by the ghost of a gaunt old man walking from the area of James Madison School and to the Stone Academy and knocking on their windows.

Perry County

***Otterbein United Methodist
Church Cemetery
The Grave of Mary Henry***
*County Road 62/ Otterbein
Road NW
Rushville, Ohio 43150
39.77194, -82.36333*

Bloody Horseshoe Grave

*Otterbein Church
and Cemetery.*

James Kennedy Henry was a farmer and early settler born in 1814. In 1844, two women caught his eye—Mary Angle and Rachael Hodge. Both were attractive and charming, and James was so smitten with both, he could not decide which one to marry. One night while heading home from visiting his sweethearts, he fell to sleep on the saddle of his horse. When he awakened, the horse was standing outside the door of Mary Angle.

James took it as a sign—fate had decided Mary would be his bride. The two were married on a chilly day of January 11th, 1844. It was a tradition for the parents of the bride and groom to give them a gift they could use in their new life as a couple. Such, the newlyweds received one handsome workhorse from Mary's parents and one workhorse from James' parents, so the two had a team of horses to start a farm.

Mary and James were happy together for a little more than a year until Mary died giving birth to their first child. In February of 1845, James buried her in a corner plot at the local Otterbein Cemetery. Distraught, the widowed man would do everything he could to forget Mary—throwing himself into his farming trying desperately to rebuild his life. But there was one thing James did not do. He did not return the horse Mary's parents had given the couple on their wedding day.

Mary's grave.

James took nearly three years before he would begin courting his earlier sweetheart, Rachael Hodge. During this time, in the surrounding area, some whispered that James had broken tradition by not returning the horse to Mary's parents after she died. Mary's family was having a difficult time making ends meet and needed the horse for their farm. There were hard feelings between the families not spoken aloud.

Rachael was only 22-years-old when she took James' hand in marriage. All would seem perfect except for one small thing occurring when James visited his first wife's grave not long after taking his new bride. He noted on the back of Mary's headstone, the bloody red shape of a horseshoe! It was an omen that would always linger in the back of his mind for many years. James and Rachael had four daughters and were married for nearly 11 years. Happy, the couple were, but the dark cloud of the horseshoe grave followed James wherever he went.

The Bloody Horseshoe Grave.

Then the inevitable happened. The curse would come full swing. While working in the barn one Friday evening, he was kicked in the head by a horse and instantly killed. It was the very horse James had not returned to Mary's parents that put him in the grave.

To this day, the bloody horseshoe print is still marking the grave. Visitors to the cemetery have seen lights and even heard the sound of horses roaming around the graves. Yet no farm animals have been around.

Pike County

Pike Lake State Park
Pike Lake Road
Bainbridge, Ohio 45612
39.159920, -83.218545

The Haunted Stump

Back in the olden days, when someone needed to clear land for a house or a field, all the neighbors for miles around would come together and help out. They would cut the trees down to stumps, chop them into logs, and with handspikes, roll them into a pile, and have a bonfire. It was called a "log rolling," and it was a time of picnics and festivities for the whole community. All the while, they took turns tending the fires. Once in a while, a spark would fly, or a flame would lick the hem of a shirt or dress.

At one particular log burning in the 1860s where Pike Lake State Park is now, a young woman of about 18 years of age was working with the others poking and prodding the limbs and branches to keep the fire strong and the wood burning, easing her way around one fire when a huge, flaming log broke loose from the top of the pile and careened downward. As she had her stick in her hand, the log rolled on it so the young woman keeled inward, and she could not release her fingers. She fell forward and was dragged to the earth until her palms slapped hard on the ground. The burning log rolled right over her hands and to her wrists.

Help came quickly, but not fast enough. The girl's hands were so severely burned, as she was wringing them, they fell right off and on to a stump. She died, and for years after, those passing the stump would see two charred ghost hands rising from the stump or feel their hot grasp on their ankles as they walked by.

Great Buzzard's Rock/Big Rock
Big Rock Cabins - Private
Cabins
4348 Big Run Road
Beaver, Ohio 45613
39.098067,-82.775932

The Legend of Old Raridan, Last Ohio Wolf

Raridan's lair.

In the late 1700s, when settlers flooded into Ohio, the wolves that still roamed the last of the wild areas began to starve as the land was cleared for farming. In desperation, many wolves started to prey upon the animals in the farming communities. One of those was a large pack with a leader the hunters named Raridan. He was the scapegoat the farmers searched out, the one the angry hunters could never catch, but always, they swore to each other they would be the one to bring the dreadful culprit down.

It was one dark day when the battle between settlers and wolves came head to head. The farmers began to hunt the wolves down using hounds to pursue them mercilessly. The wolves began to retreat to a rocky knob of high cliffs, known for the bones of animals littered along its ledges and slopes as old and sick animals went there to die. It was not long until all the wolves but Old Raridan and his mate were dead, and hounds circled them near a place called Great Buzzard's Rock.

Old Raridan's mate was mortally wounded, and he dragged her limp body back to their lair on the rocks. Just as they eased along the long summit trail, an explosion rang out, and the she-wolf was brought down in a single shot.

Soon after, Old Raridan must have known his time was due. He stood his ground, came eye to eye with those who had taken all he had known, his family, his life. Another shot rang out, forcing Old Raridan to keel sideways as his back and legs were ripped by gunshot. He forced himself to his feet and again stared his attackers in the eye, barely able to stand. But the guns fell to the hunters' sides. Only a moment lapsed when Old Raridan leaned down, grabbed his mate by the back of the neck. He pulled her along the trail and toward the peak of the huge rock. He vanished then, never to be seen again with a miserable and haunting howl. However, for at least 150 years, stories have been passed down that Old Raridan's ghost haunts Great Buzzard's Rock, now called Big Rock, his cry still heard resonating against the small caves and crevices. Those passing by see shadows of wolves on the walls and bones at the peak.

Sandusky County

Bridge over Muddy Creek
2903 Fought Road
Lindsey, Ohio 43442
41.422921, -83.201654

The Elmore Rider

The bridge as it appeared in yesteryears. Courtesy of the Harris-Elmore Public Library, Grace Luebke Local History Collection.

There is a ghost light about 30 miles from Toledo near the towns of Lindsey and Oak Harbor. Old legends relate a house was haunted by an old man who shot himself. He threatened beforehand to haunt the place. A later story explains the lights with more romantic flair—it is about a couple who pledged their love to each other just as World War I broke out. The young man was sent off to war and fought overseas. The two wrote back and forth for a year, long letters of love and heartache, and missing each other, then the letters from the man simply stopped coming. Heartbroken, the young woman was sure her sweetheart was dead.

It would be March 21st of 1918 when he returned from the war. Why he had not written his sweetheart, is not told. But to surprise the young woman as he neared her home, he shut off his motorcycle along the roadway the evening of his return and snuck to her window and peered inside. To his shock and dismay, the woman he thought pledged her life to him was with another man. Distraught, the young man sped off on his motorcycle down the road, not heeding his speed, nor ruts in the old farm road. Suddenly, the bike hitched, and he tumbled off near a small bridge over Muddy Creek. He flew from his bike and was decapitated by barbed fence wire running along the fields. Now, legends tell that on March 21st each year, the Elmore Rider returns. People see ghostly lights along Fought Road, where it crosses Muddy Creek.

A ghostly motorcycle rider is seen near the towns of Lindsey and Elmore, the aftermath of a broken pledge of love.
The story has been around for a while. The article below comes from the Cleveland Plain Dealer November 24th, 1922.

"GHOST LIGHT" SHINING

Port Clinton Mystery Renewed; Curious Go Miles to See It.

(Plain Dealer Special)

PORT CLINTON. O., Nov. 23.—The so-called "Ghost Light" which appears at night on the road between Lindsey and Oak Harbor, and is attracting the attention of Port Clinton residents.

They are making trips to the spot where the light has been reported to have made its nocturnal appearance for many years. Atmospheric conditions, it is said, cause the light to be more brilliant at times.

Its mysterious appearance and disappearance have caused many to drive for miles to witness this spectacular illusion

Tindall Bridge
*Corner of South River Road
and Rice Road
Fremont, Ohio 43420
41.308406,-83.157842*

The Haunting of Hard Luck Bridge

At times, witnesses have heard strange groans and screams at Tindall Bridge over the Sandusky River near Fremont. A ghostly figure wanders beneath its skeletal frame. The hauntings are believed to come from the ghastly deeds committed nearby the bridge in the past. Built in 1915, the bridge was constructed to replace another washed out by floods in 1913. It is made of steel now and is high above the water.

Somebody along the line nicknamed it the Hard Luck Bridge, not just because it kept getting knocked over from floods. There have been deadly accidents there and a suicide. Then, in May of 1955, 29-year-old Shirley Bradford, a waitress at the open-all-night Hut Restaurant in Fremont, was abducted at work by gunpoint by a Samuel Tannyhill. He took $100.00 and forced her into his car. When Missus Bradford told him she recognized him and threatened to tell the police, he took her to the Tindall Bridge and murdered her. Her body was found by two farmers crossing the bridge the next morning. Tannyhill later died in the electric chair. His victim walks the shores.

Scioto County

Shawnee State Forest
Dead Man Hollow
13291 US-52
(State Forest Road 2)
West Portsmouth, Ohio 45633
38.698616, -83.237139

Mysterious Grave

The mysterious grave.

A mysterious grave lies deep within a hollow near Portsmouth. It is in an area of a dense, dark forest in a secluded pocket of Shawnee State Forest tucked between Little Gum Hollow and Webb Hollow on the right fork of Twin Creek. In the 1930s, CCC laborers working on the forest roadway found bones. Wedged within the crevice of a small rock overhang nearby were combs, implements, and tin plates—the type of things a peddler would trade along with the tools he would use for repairs around the remote homes he stopped in on his way. The remains were later moved and reburied adjacent to the little cleft in the rocks.

A stone was set along the right fork of Twin Creek in the hollow to commemorate the peddler. It read: "H. T. Aug. 13, 1824. A. D., Dead M." Upon finding the bones, old folks began to recall talk of a peddler who, in the 1820s, routinely visited the rural towns nearby and who had oddly ceased calling on farms on his usual route. They remembered hearing that a peddling tinker had paused in the village of Buena Vista in Scioto County along the Ohio River. He was directed, after selling his wares, along a 6-hour rugged footpath northeast to the settlement of Upper Turkey Creek, a community about three miles north of the town of Friendship. He never got to his destination.

Most believed the peddler was ambushed and murdered, but no one knew the truth about how he died, or at least they would not tell. For many years, locals avoided the area of the hollow after dark reporting ghostly screams, whistling, and strange noises. After many years, floodwaters along the Twin Creek washed the grave away, and a bag of trinkets scattered nearby was discovered.

Vinton County

Moonville Tunnel
Hope-Moonville Road
McArthur, Ohio 45651
39.307008, -82.321342
Parking:
39.308256, -82.324371

That's Mine—The Drunken Brakeman

Moonville Tunnel.

Many years ago, a young brakeman collected his pay. He had worked hard all week and decided that his hard labor was worthy of a good, hard drink in town. So on his way home, he stopped in at the local tavern in Zaleski. But one drink led to another until he was so drunk, he could barely walk.

Sometime after dark, he left the bar with a bottle in hand and began to walk the tracks toward home. Partway, he determined he was due a short nap and laid down on the stones still warm from the day's sun and rested his head on a rise. As he fell fast to sleep, the bottle slipped from his fingers. But unfortunately, he did not contemplate that the rocks for his bed were the ballast from the train track, and his pillow was a rail, and during the night, a train passed through.

The next day, a miner walking the tracks spotted the bottle lying near a railroad tie and reached down to pick it up. There were droplets of blood not far away. He heard a low moaning, "That's mine." Looking around, the startled man saw nobody nearby but followed the bloody trail to the brush near the tracks. He found the young man's dead body, mashed by the train.

After, locals would recall seeing the young brakeman staggering along the tracks just after the tunnel and before the first trestle. He would pause, waver there a moment before crumpling into a heap on the railroad ties. But before he fell, he would drop something peculiar to the ground. Then he would disappear altogether. Some were curious enough to search out the ghost and try to determine what had fallen from his fingers. When they investigated the place the item had dropped, a voice would seep from the brush, "That's mine."

Washington County

Beverly Lock
Ohio Street
Beverly, Ohio 45715
39.546197,-81.642129

Ghostly Echoes of the Ill-fated Buckeye Belle

Beverly Lock today.

On November 12th of 1852, the Buckeye Belle riverboat was making its way along the Muskingum River at Beverly, Ohio with 40 passengers when a boiler exploded at the gates of Lock 4. Twenty-four people were killed, and some bodies were never recovered. On foggy, rainy November evenings, if you listen hard along the river at the lock, you can hear the sounds of the men working on the riverboat that fateful autumn day back in 1852. Some have listened to ghostly riverboat whistles, but the source of the sound is never found.

Anchorage House
*(aka Putnam Villa/Douglas
Putnam House)
498 George Street
Marietta, Ohio 45750
39.413551, -81.463473*

Floating Eliza

In the 1850s, it took ten years for Douglas Putnam to build this home for his wife, Eliza. It cost an extravagant $65,000, but Eliza had to have it. Eliza fell in love with a friend's home during a visit to New Jersey, and it became the model for her own house in Marietta. It has twenty-two rooms and a tower room with a widow's walk. The Italian villa has sandstone walls quarried from neighboring hills and overlooks the city of Marietta and both the Ohio and Muskingum Rivers.

It was initially called "Putnam Place," and not until it changed hands later, was it deemed 'The Anchorage House.' It hosted many functions for the well-to-do of Marietta. Eliza passed away in September of 1862 from heart disease, only three years after the initial construction of the home. She was 53-years-old. It remained in the family until a couple of years after Douglas died, and his third wife sold it to the Harry Knox family, owners of Knox Boatyard. They renamed it the Anchorage. The Anchorage changed hands several times before it became a nursing home for about fifty patients in 1960 and renamed The Christian Anchorage. By 1984, all the patients had moved to the more modern Marie Antoinette Pavilion right next door. When it was a nursing home, patients, nurses, and aides would see a shadowy woman on the stairs near the dining room. One nurse also reported seeing a woman in period clothing walking from the stairway to the dining area. And on another occasion, an aide also saw a phantom light wiggling its way across the widow's walk on top. Eliza's ghost has been seen both inside the home and outside.

While hiking one afternoon in Zaleski, I came upon a couple who visited the home one afternoon and were more than happy to tell me their story of the Anchorage House. It seems that after pulling into the graveled side road to the Anchorage, they got out of their cars. Just as the woman turned to head toward the building, she stopped in utter horror. Not a stone's throw away was a full-bodied apparition of a woman floating several feet above the grassy lawn!

Wood County

Fort Meigs
857 W Indiana Avenue
Perrysburg, Ohio 43551
41.550053,-83.65164

Dark Apparitions

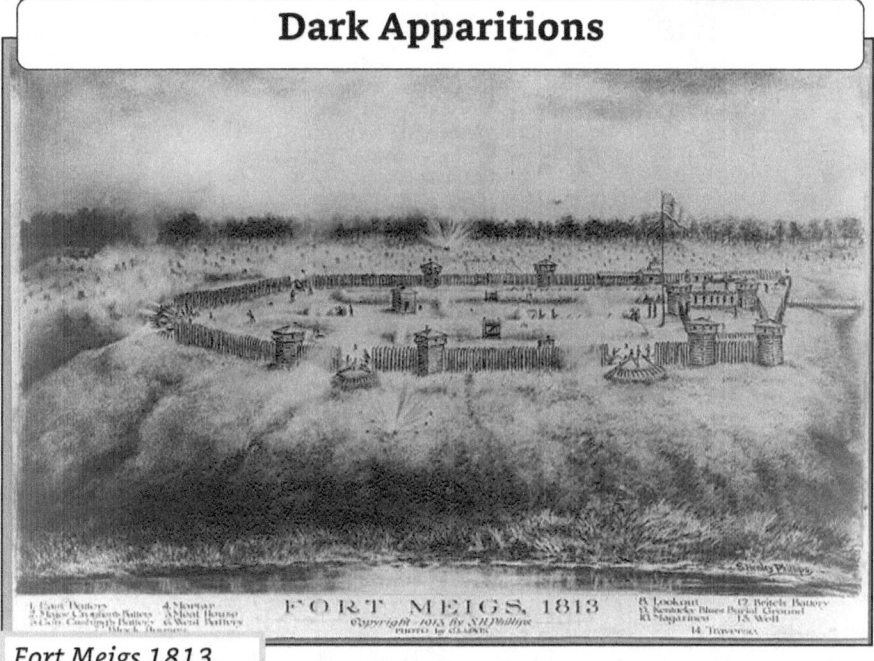

Fort Meigs 1813.

Fort Meigs was a fortification along the Maumee River in Ohio during the War of 1812. There are three unmarked cemeteries at the fort, and many soldiers were buried in mass graves. Travelers passing the property hear cannon and gunfire at night. Dark apparitions have been seen walking the area and along the hillside leading to the Maumee River.

Holcomb Road
Pemberville, Ohio 43450
41.340769, -83.484578

The Legend of Holcomb Woods

Holcomb Road—the place of legends, ghosts, and dead children.

There is a legend not far from Bowling Green. A school bus driver was taking a full load of children home for the day, and the route took them through a thickly-treed area along Holcomb Road. Suddenly the bus veered off the pavement and smashed into a tree. The driver perished instantly. The bus exploded, and all within died a fiery death. If you drive along the road, you can see the bus driver's face on the tree that was the scene of the bus crash. Two ghostly white lights will rush toward you from the far end of the road with the sound of children screaming, vanishing at the tree.

**Wood County
Historical Center**
*13660 County Home Road
Bowling Green, Ohio 43402
41.350333,-83.615398*

Sunset Acres

The Wood County Infirmary was built in 1869 on about 160 acres outside Bowling Green. Authorities set it up as a self-sufficient farm. If inmates were physically able, they were expected to work on the farmland, including feeding and care of the animals, gardening, and food preparation. Some tended to other patients and completed the upkeep of the poor house. The infirmary's Sunset Acres cemetery has been on the property for one hundred years. Those passing by in cars have reported tiny lights dancing and weaving over the graves, and as in the image above, apparitions.

Haunted Colleges

Ohio University
Jefferson Hall
E Union Street
Athens, Ohio 45701
39.327227,-82.09641

She Floated

Jefferson Hall is located on East Green at Ohio University. It was built in 1956 and opened in 1958. It was used as a dining hall and residence hall originally housing female students.

In 1996, a group of students exploring the upstairs came upon a room with the door open. Just after peering inside, they immediately noticed a woman sitting at a desk in a far corner of the room. She was apparently 'transparent and floating above the chair' before she vanished. Lights and curling irons have turned on by themselves and ghostly figures roam the hallways. Students living in the dorms have even heard the sound of marbles rolling across the ceiling.

Columbus State Community College Grounds
550 E Spring Street
Columbus, Ohio 43215
39.968372,-82.986517

College Above the City of the Dead

There have been complaints of strange noises and lights flickering at the college campus. Most of the events happen at night and both security officers and patrolmen in the area have been startled by disturbances they cannot explain. *It can be explained.* There was once a Catholic cemetery on the grounds of the college with approximately 4000 burials between 1846 and 1874. Eventually, a new cemetery was developed farther outside the city, and those with family buried here were asked to move their dead kin. Some did. But not all were moved before, in 1905, St. Patrick's College was plopped on the hallowed ground. And later, Columbus State Community College.

Bowling Green State University
Eva Marie Saint Theatre
Bowling Green, Ohio 43403
41.375645, -83.639265

The Curse of Alice

Legends say that the mysterious ghost of a student actor named Alice haunts the building. While portraying Desdemona in a performance of Othello, a prop fell from a rafter above the theatre stage, killing the young woman. Since then, the cast and crew officially invite Alice to all performances, and a seat is left vacant for her. If these actions are not fulfilled, Alice causes objects to fly during the performance, and an accident will occur.

Ohio State University
Orton Hall
155 South Oval Mall
Columbus, Ohio 43210
39.998402,-83.011903

Lonely Lantern Light

Orton Hall was named after Ohio State's first president and a professor of Geology from 1873-1899, Doctor Edward Orton. Orton enjoyed reading by lantern light in the tower. Even though he is long-dead, students have seen the lights from his ghostly lantern flickering through the slots.

Citations

Allen County:
News-Medical.Net - History of TBLibrary of Congress print—LC-USZ62-23226, HABS NJ,10-GLGA.V,1A--18 | HABS NJ,10-GLGA.V,1A--18
Lima Daily News - Friday, Oct 10, 1890, Lima, Ohio IS IT A GHOST? A Strange Visitation That is Exciting The North End, Column 3, page 4
Athens County:
Supernatural Athens: One of the Scariest Places on Earth" Caitlin Kight
http://www.forgottenoh.com/News/athensfox.html
http://homepages.rootsweb.ancestry.com/~tfisher/hocking/hvhchap14.htm
Cemeteries:
http://www.wolfereunion.com/History.htm - Joe & Barb Wolfe Rader
Delaware County:
Red Slipper Murder:
Portsmouth Times - Wednesday, September 23, 1953, Portsmouth, Ohio
Mansfield News Journal - Saturday, September 26, 1953, Mansfield, Ohio
Charleston Gazette - Sunday, October 10, 1954, Charleston, West Virginia
Sharon Wick exclusively for Ohio Genealogy Express ©2008 http://www.ohiogenealogyexpress.com/delaware/delco_hist_orange.htm
Perkins:
University Men See Telescope - Mansfield News, The - Tuesday, June 08, 1926, Manfield,
Perkins Observatory Memorial Is Result of One Man's Idea - Sandusky Star Journal - Wednesday, August 19, 1925, Sandusky, Ohio
Ohio Wesleyan University's Astronomy Club - Student Observatory History- http://cc.owu.edu/~starweb/history.html
Perkins Observatory- Ohio Wesleyan University. http://www.perkins-observatory.org/
Strand Theatre :
http://www.thestrandtheatre.net/
http://www.ohioexploration.com/delawarecounty.htm
Railway:
Library of Congress Prints and Photographs Division Washington, D.C. 20540 USA- LC-USZ62-132007 (b&w film copy neg.), LC-USZ62-132007
Franklin County:
Berliner Park:
http://www.historicmapworks.com/Overlay/?m=73596&c=US&lat=39.972532&lng=-83.004348
Camp Chase:
The National magazine: an illustrated monthly, Volume 46, Let's Talk This Over—Info on Ransburg
The Washington Post, June 16, 1917 page 5, Veiled Lady of Camp Chase," Dramatic Figure of Reunion, Wildly Cheered by Dixie's Sons
Library of Congress: LC-DIG-ppmsca-15835
Fire Museum:
Special thanks to Bill Hall Retired Firefighter and fire department historian for Columbus, Columbus Fire Department History 1822-2012.
Library of Congress Prints and Photographs LOT 10869
Evening Gazette - Wednesday, May 07, 1919, Xenia, Ohio - Columbus Fire Mounts to Nine
Elyria Chronicle -May 6, 1919 - A Disastrous Fire Sweeps Columbus May 6
Columbus Health Department:
Columbus Public Health Department - Ohio School for the Blind
Columbus Public Health, 240 Parsons Avenue Columbus, Ohio 43215http://publichealth.columbus.gov/columbus-public-health-history.aspx
Dictionary of Ohio Historic Places Somerset Publishers Inc, Editorial Staff
Ohio Exploration Society - http://www.ohioexploration.com/franklincounty.htm
William Martin, History of Franklin County: A Collection of Reminiscences of the Early Settlement of the County (Columbus, 1858).

Ohio Statehouse:
Amarillo Globe-Times - Monday, October 03, 1960, Amarillo, Texas
A Story of Kate Chase's Family - By Paul LeRoy Hacker p 14
http://www.thisweeknews.com/content/stories/germanvillage/
news/2009/09/30/1001geghost_ln.html
Library of Congress Prints - Kate Chase image-Abraham Lincoln image
and Mary Tod Lincoln image - Brady-Handy Collection Funeral
Procession - Creator(s): Ehrgott, Forbriger & Co., Ruger, A. , artist
Deaf School:
Ohio School for the Deaf - http://www.ohioschoolforthedeaf.org/
history.aspx
Bloody Island and British Island:
The fight that forged Ohio - Often overlooked, War of 1812 secured state's
future - he Dispatch Printing Company
http://theshadowlands.net/places/ohio.htm
image of soldiers: Wyrdlight
Historic Cemeteries:
South and East:
http://www.genealogybug.net/Franklin_Cemeteries/city_graveyards/
page037.htm and
The Columbus City Graveyards Content © 1985 by Donald M. Schlegel
Camp Chase Articles Southeast Cemetery Transfer to Camp Chase -
Information compiled by Dennis Ranney
*http://www.genealogybug.net/Franklin_Cemeteries/city_graveyards/
page007.htm*
Lincoln Funeral Train:
The Lincoln Highway National Museum & Archives 102 Old Lincoln Way
West Galion, Ohio 44833
Above Top Secret: Ghostly Lincoln Funeral Train http://
www.abovetopsecret.com/forum/thread107433/pg1
Gallia County
Sandusky Daily Register - Monday, January 20, 1890, Sandusky, Ohio -
The Lake Erie Ghost That Haunts the Railroad Track
Lima Daily News - Wednesday, January 15, 1890, Lima, Ohio- WELSH'S
HEADLESS BODY -What is Driving Men From a Freight Run http://
www.forgottenoh.com/Counties/Hancock/ctyrd4cemetery.html
Logansport Daily Pharos, Tuesday Evening March 22, 1892 - *HORRIBLY
HURT IN A WRECK. A Fireman Receives Injuries That Will Probably Kill
Him.*
*The Daily Times - LIMA OHIO TUESDAY, MARCH 22 1892 - Cannon Ball
Train Wrecked*
Hancock County:
Image of Conductor: Library of Congress: LC-USW3-010642-E, Delano,
Jack, photographer
Henry County
Crybaby Hill:
Grave Addiction - Graveaddiction.com

www.ingramcontent.com/pod-product-compliance
Lightning Source LLC
Chambersburg PA
CBHW020912180626
46816CB00007BA/2365